# Ghosts of the Bayou

## The Meranda Haley Series
### Book 1

JJ Lynn Daniels

B. SHEPHERD
PUBLICATIONS

Books that inspire Antifragility

# Contents

# Also by JJ Lynn Daniels

The Metal's Bane Series

Verdigris

Tarnish

Rust

*For my Father
who always believed in me*

# GHOSTS OF THE BAYOU

## THE MERANDA HALEY SERIES: BOOK ONE

## JJ LYNN DANIELS

# Chapter One

The mirror above the bar was my friend. I always positioned myself to the left side of it, where I had a clear view of the rest of the crowded room. A table about ten feet behind my right shoulder boasted a card game attended by four lesser fae. The pointed ears and powder blue skin would have gotten strange looks elsewhere in this city, but here? In Baxter's? Not a chance. A player cracked a joke about aces and those seated at his table laughed, revealing pointed teeth.

I tore my eyes from their mirth and rolled my glass between my hands. While raucous laughter filled the bar and the air hung heavy with the scent of strong drink on foul breath, this corner was an oasis. I was hardly noticed here which was just fine by me. I didn't need to sit among the horns and claws and teeth that filled the barroom. It was enough to just be near them. To not have to act too human. To be able to relax.

As a bonus, my seating choice brought me near the small dog bed on the counter where Baxter snored. The blue blanket covering the cushion had been almost completely taken over by dog hair throughout the years, but the apneic bulldog didn't seem to mind. From the way he lay there, though, seemingly boneless, I don't think he would have minded if it was a bed of bricks. He could conk out anywhere. Speaking of apnea, the dog had fallen silent. I nudged his bed until the sawing of wood resumed. *Breathe, dammit.* I would not be responsible for the bar's namesake dying on my watch.

I broke from my staring at the white and brown fur rising and falling in time with the loud snores as Charlie walking up.

"You want another one?" he asked, holding out a bottle of clear liquid.

I shook my head. "Just one tonight, Charlie. I'm teaching in the morning."

He pursed his lips, clearly unconvinced, as though whatever was on my mind required a stronger drink than the sparkling water that I nursed in the glass before me. I raised it before him in a toasting motion and took a sip.

Charlie shrugged and walked away with a muttered, "You're the boss."

I half smiled into my glass. Charlie never pressured me into purchasing hard drinks in his bar. Even better, he never asked me *why* I didn't drink any of the myriad selection of alcohol he served. It helped that I tipped well. I collected a few pretzels from the bowl Charlie had slid in front of me when I'd arrived. There was something about the salty crunch, slightly stale from the humidity, that felt like home. Maybe I spent too much time in this bar.

My eyes flashed up to the mirror again as I heard a particularly loud exclamation from the card table. My eyes slid quickly past the reflection of my olive-toned face. It was a forgettable face. Perfect for keeping a low profile in this city. Teenage me had agonized over the fact that I wasn't drop dead gorgeous like the rockstar posters that had decorated the walls of my bedroom. I had slathered myself in thick eyeliner and tried to convince fae to glamour my hair neon blue and pink.

But that was before I understood the reality of the danger I was in. The reasons my father and I hid here in this city of monsters and humans.

Now I would be hard pressed to add anything to my face to make me stand out. I'd forgone makeup for years. Just one of the many habits I'd picked up to stay secret. To keep safe.

The bar was about twenty-five feet away from the door and the barroom was scattered with individual round tables and chairs. Even with my back turned, I had plenty of time to react if someone pushed their way in who wanted to cause trouble. It helped that Baxter's was positioned on a corner near the east side of Bourbon St. on the intersection of Paulger. There were two exits from the barroom itself and at least one through the kitchen. It was as though Charlie knew his clientele. Knew that most of us wanted the security of a quick escape if we needed it.

He was considerate, for a human.

Unlike most of the humans who stayed in New Orleans and never strayed far from their mansions and their police force, Charlie didn't seem to care whether you had horns or fangs or a tail. He'd serve a paying customer and he always gave the same respect he expected from those around him.

The front door opened letting in the sounds of Bourbon Street. A jazz band doing their best to keep up with the saxophonist. Passersby laughing and dancing to the music. The scent of rain wafting in as the door gave passage.

I turned to get a better look at the newcomer. The man

who had walked in from the rain wore an oversized trench coat that covered him from neck to boot. A table near the door raised a drunken greeting at his arrival. The newcomer smiled revealing sharpened canines and adjusted his trajectory toward them.

*Bloodsucker,* the part of me that hung out with humans too often, whispered in my mind. The vampire took the proffered seat at the table and shrugged his coat off throwing drops of water across the well-worn floorboards. He waved Charlie over to order a drink. *Bloody Mary, anyone?*

Not a threat to me.

Not here.

The baseball bat across from me drew my eye. It was studded with sharpened nails and lived permanently on the shelf behind the bar. Charlie kept a tight hold on the peace of this place.

I was about to return my attention to scratch behind Baxter's ears when I noticed the woman. She drifted in just as the door was closing. Her dress wasn't made for the late August rainfall. It hung from her pale shoulders in gauzy whisps as though it was made to be a nightgown rather than a protection against inclement weather. Her dark hair hung to her waist, tangles throughout its mass as she swung her head from side to side, searching the room for *something*.

The hairs at the nape of my neck prickled, standing at attention. The rest of the patrons ignored her, not one looking her direction. I understood. On Bourbon Street these days, it was safer to ignore anything out of the ordinary and pray desperately that it would ignore you too. If any of the beings in the barroom even *could* see her.

I followed suit, plastering my eyes down to my glass which was sweating unhelpfully in the humidity. The feeling of unease grew, and I knew the woman was getting closer. She couldn't hurt me, not here, I told myself. If I kept my eyes down, she wouldn't even notice me.

A rush of cold at my back.

She was right behind me.

The sounds of the bar faded to a dull roaring in my ears as my every sense attuned itself to her presence. Her aura clung to me like hands grasping at my arms, at my hair, pulling my very being in her direction. I clenched my jaw and focused on breathing normally. My eyesight blurred from the effort to control myself and my glass swam before me.

"I know you can see me." Her whisper was sharp in my ear drums, as though her voice was *inside* my head.

She couldn't know that. She was bluffing, certainly. But she drew me to her. Her voice like a siren to my soul whispered that I could turn around and talk to her, ask her what was wrong. I had been created to protect the humans from these beings. Resisting her call was a physical pain. A hand clenched around my heart. But turning around would be far worse. I had experience with that too.

The chill from her presence ran down my arms. My hands numbed. I couldn't feel the glass that I clenched so tightly a part of me wondered if it would shatter.

A cool breath on my neck.

My heart sped up as the woman leaned closer. I resisted the urge to shudder.

If I moved, she would know that I couldn't ignore her and the consequences of that—

"Are you sure you don't want a refill?" Charlie's voice drew my attention, and the pressure was gone. I spared a glance toward the mirror and saw that the woman had disappeared. Vanished as though she'd never been in the room at all. The sounds of the bar crashed into my senses like a physical blow. The humid warmth of the room settled the hairs down on my arms and the back of my neck. I was never so grateful for the New Orleans humidity.

I gave Charlie what I hoped was a believable smile and raised my glass. "Maybe I will."

Like any good bartender, Charlie could read people, so it didn't surprise me when he settled himself at my end of the bar after pouring my second glass. He must have seen how shaken I was even if he didn't understand why. He busied himself cleaning a spot off the bar with a rag that he kept tucked into his apron and didn't pry. Another good trait in a bartender.

"My dad's giving me the Agency," I told him. Finally saying out loud the words that had been screaming in my head all night.

Charlie raised an eyebrow, the only confirmation that he had heard me as he leaned in toward the spot on the counter and gave it another violent treatment with the rag.

"I don't know what I'm going to do." I raised the glass to my lips, grimacing at the bitter sparkling taste.

"You could keep it," Charlie offered, pulling a spray bottle from under the counter and dousing the offending section of the bar top.

I shook my head. I'd left that life long ago. The fact that my father had the gall to *give* me the place rubbed me the wrong way. Especially after the way we'd left things.

"You could sell it." Charlie found a more abrasive brush and went at the spot with a vengeance.

I shook my head again. The Agency was thousands of dollars in debt. Only an idiot would take it on as a project. Or an unlucky daughter of a man prone to working *pro bono* more often than not. Dad's empathy at the expense of all sense was one of the main causes of our arguments.

"You could stay here and drink instead of dealing with it." Charlie pulled out what appeared to be a makeshift flame thrower before seeing my face and deciding against using it.

I raised my glass toward him. "That's the best option I've been able to come up with too."

"You're always welcome here, Meranda." Charlie said, finally abandoning his anti-spot ministrations and turning to face me.

I searched for words to convey my gratitude. I knew that was true, Charlie always made me feel welcome. He even poured my sparkling water from an unmarked bottle so none of the rest of the patrons knew I wasn't drinking. His courtesy was unmatched anywhere else in the city. Despite the differences in our looks, I always felt more at home in this barroom among the horns and claws and teeth than I did among the humans.

"I just wish some time you'd bring someone with you who *would* drink something else," Charlie muttered and dumped a fresh set of pretzels into the bowl before me. "I make a mean ale and you've never said a single compliment about it."

I laughed, a natural sound in this place. It dispelled the rest of the chill the woman had left in her wake. "I'll keep it in mind, Charlie. I'm sure your ale is life changing."

# Chapter Two

"Ms. Haley, how can we be sure the portals won't open again?" The slight red-headed boy in the front row asked. Jean Doucet. His father owned one of the major companies that maintained the streetcar lines that ran through the city and, more importantly, the ley lines beneath.

A few of the other students snickered at the question.

One particularly bold student, Damian Calzo, muttered, "Shut up, nerd."

There were kids like that in every class that I had taught. I shot him a silencing look before responding. Jean's comment had gotten the attention of most of the other students in the class, and their eyes were locked on me as I returned to the front of the room.

"Well, Jean, there's no reason to think that they won't. In fact, there have been reports coming from the West Coast for years that they are still being surprised by portals opening almost every month."

A few gasps made me want to walk back my statement, but I couldn't. It was true.

"While we haven't had portals open near us in almost fifty years, we're still maintaining precautions for them. We still wouldn't dare put an airplane in the sky."

The last time air travel was a normal part of human life was close to seventy-five years ago. It only took a few portals opening in the sky and winged monsters flying through for the humans to decide that ground travel was safer. I doubted half these students had even seen *pictures* of airplanes at this point.

"Not to mention the Rift..." A small voice piped up from the corner of the room. Lily White, an unnecessarily poetic name, but when your parents own the company that builds houses on Mansion Row, you can get away with nonsense like that.

A shudder passed through the class at that comment, and I gave it a moment to sink in. The children were right to be afraid. The Rift opened around the time the portals first began to appear, but while the portals were sporadic, closing almost as quickly as they had opened, the Rift remained. It spread, like a cancer across the land and the beings that crawled out of it —

"The Rift is thousands of miles away," I told them, "And of far less consequence to your lives this week than your history test will be if you don't study. So—" I clapped my hands, startling a few of the students who were daydreaming too vividly about the Rift and its monsters. "Study time. Pull out your book and notes. You can study in groups or alone, just keep the noise down to a dull roar."

The students scrambled into groups whose dynamics were sure to stifle any chance of work being accomplished, and I settled into the wheeled chair behind the teacher's desk.

The teacher whose class I was substituting had left the

vague lesson plan of, 'test Friday, make them study'. I couldn't blame her. I wouldn't spend the time spelling out work for my substitute if I was assuredly dying of the stomach flu either. Ms. Holden was a well-known hypochondriac, but I didn't complain. It meant more work for a substitute teacher like me, so three cheers for whatever major ailment would take her down next.

I was just marking down the attendance when I felt it. A chill crept over me. The hairs on the back of my neck stood on end.

Something had entered the room.

Twice in two days was a bad sign.

I set my pen down and looked up. The students were mostly quiet, whispering excitedly to one another about whatever gossip takes up more of a high schooler's life than it should. I didn't see anything lurking in the corners of the room, but the temperature was plummeting around my desk. A student at the desk nearest me shrugged his jacket back on mid-conversation. They had no idea what was in this room with them, I realized. That probably left them safe.

Safer than I was anyway.

"I know you can see me." The whisper hit me like the shock of jumping into freezing water.

It was behind me.

I knew these beings. I knew their tricks, but still the apparition startled me.

I jumped.

A light laugh sounded from behind me, mirthless, callous and cruel.

"Gotcha."

There are a few rules when it comes to the spirits of those who have passed on. I'd learned them long ago. Those who do not believe the paranormal exists, rarely see it. That has been true for centuries. Part of the reason why the unbeliever is safe is because they are so busy *reasoning* through why whatever phenomenon they witness *can't* be a ghost. Ghosts are emboldened by those who interact with them. They crave it. They thrive off of it. Every interaction they receive makes them stronger, more corporeal. And I should have known better.

My arm nearly froze as the ghost laid its hand on my right shoulder.

"What do you want?" I whispered, trying not to draw the attention of the students in the class.

"You ignored me last night."

I remembered the woman in the barroom. I could picture her in my mind's eye, and I knew that if I turned around, I would see her again.

"Don't take it personally, I ignore almost everyone."

The light laugh sounded again, and the hand drew back before settling on my opposite shoulder. The woman leaned in, her dark hair spilling over my hand that was gripping the edge of the desk so hard my knuckles were white.

"You speak so flippantly, when you have so much to lose."

It wasn't the first time I had been threatened by the dearly departed. But the way that the hand on my shoulder gestured toward the classroom before me, I knew she was threatening the students. My stomach clenched. I couldn't let that stand.

I stood, rolling my chair behind me with such speed I heard an oomph as the half-corporeal being took a chair back to the gut.

"Students," I called out. "Class is dismissed for the day;

you may continue your studying in the lunchroom if you need."

"But Miss," Jean began. "We still have fifteen minutes left."

I was suddenly feeling a strange camaraderie with the Damian kid whose eyes looked murderous.

"Then I guess you have time to walk *very slowly* to your next class." I poured some level of command into my voice and jerked a chin toward the door. "Get out."

An almost preternatural speed took over the room and the students were gone in a blink.

Once the last student had left, I finally turned to look over my visitor. She appeared exactly as I had remembered from last night. The same gauzy dressing gown barely draped her thin frame. Her hair hung tangled down to her waist and her dark eyes were red rimmed and glassy, almost as though they were swimming with tears

This ghost must have been dead for a while to be as powerful as she was. She had to have interacted with humans for years to be able to lay a hand on me after only one encounter.

"What's your name?" I asked. If there's anything I've learned about older ghosts, it's that they like to talk, and they *love* to talk about themselves.

"Sarah," she said, raising her chin as though she had just declared herself to be some kind of queen. The air sucked out of the room, and I held what little remained in my lungs.

The vacuum that took over the room was oppressive. A pressure built in my chest. Sarah had a decent amount of power to impact her environment this fully. I could feel my lungs constricting, craving oxygen.

"How did you die, Sarah?" I gasped out.

The apparition flinched as the memory of her demise hit her anew. The edges of her being flickered in and out of physicality. She coughed once and a foul liquid splattered the floor. Water leaked from the side of her mouth, tinging red as blood followed. Now she was at the disadvantage. I could breathe again.

"What do you want from me?" I asked.

Some of her confidence was drained, or perhaps she was just exhausting herself with the effort to hold herself in this plane.

"I have a message for you," she whispered, a gurgle sounding behind it. "From your father."

"Don't be ridiculous," I snapped, "I can talk to my father whenever I want."

I had a short fuse for ghost shenanigans. Sue me.

The woman flickered once more; her whole body shuddered as she forced herself to stay present. She opened her mouth once. More pink water rushed out, and she closed it.

"You are meant for so much more than you believe," she finally managed.

I nearly blinked. That almost did sound like a message from my father. But ghosts this old were notorious liars, and I didn't have time for it.

"Thanks for the pep talk," I said, then I poured the power I'd been gifted into my voice. "Begone."

I dismissed her with a wave of my hand and with one last startled face, she vanished.

I pushed a shaking fist into my desk and sagged against it. I'd really muffed it up this time. It wasn't just individual ghosts who were emboldened by people talking with them. Every ghost I encountered for the next week would know I had talked with one of them, and they too would be drawn to me.

I pushed the chair under the desk and turned out the lights. I had to re-ward the school now, which was inconvenient at best. I couldn't have spirits visiting the classrooms when I was trying to teach.

It was very distracting.

I pushed my way into the busy hallway and left the chilled classroom behind. The bell had rung a few minutes earlier and the hall was filled with uniformed children racing toward their lockers or the bathrooms or their next classes. The sound and scent of test anxiety and teenage hormones crashed into me. No part of me missed this stage of life.

I wasn't a great deal taller than most of the students, and I was practically dwarfed by the older boys. I stuck near the wall to avoid being crushed and swept away in the tide of blue and white plaid.

The floor was a dark wood, somehow impervious to scuff marks despite the years of harsh treatment it had received. I was certain there was some expensive concoction used by a cleaning crew each evening to keep the floorboards looking so perfect and the windows so clear. The French windows I passed gave a stunning view of the rose garden in front of the building. The fountain was happily spouting water despite the rain that threatened to overfill it. The stone saint whose name I had not learned dutifully stood guard over the rosebushes and stone pathways that led to the wrought iron gate and the street beyond.

I didn't have another class for the day, but I was reticent to venture out into the rainstorm just yet.

"Meranda Haley,"

My full name drew my attention, and I looked up to

find the master-at-arms making a beeline toward me. The tartan tsunami of students parted before his massive frame as he pushed his way through them.

Geoff Harnock was built like a mountain. The sparsely-worded instructor biography on the school's website told me that he had spent many years pursuing mercenary work with the Rangers before finally settling in New Orleans. He had a daughter here at the Academy when he retired from Ranger work, and the faculty had been looking for a new weapons instructor, so he took the job.

He kept the brown hair atop his head buzzed short, but his well-trimmed beard was peppered with gray. His face was hardened, deeply lined by difficult times and sun exposure riding in the wilderness, hunting the things that crawled out of the portals to threaten the humans. Despite his granite exterior, the wrinkles around his eyes betrayed the good humor and smiles that so easily graced his face. His blue eyes twinkled as he shot me one of those smiles now.

"Master Harnock," I greeted him. "How goes the weapons training today?"

"Bah!" Geoff said. "The kids are almost hopeless, but I'll whip 'em into shape."

I laughed. Geoff Harnock never had a kind thing to say about the students who worked with him, least of all his daughter, Artemis. According to him, they were all inches from certain death if they did not practice with their weapons at least twice as often as they studied. I didn't bother to tell him that they didn't study that often either, so his time spent with them could almost amount to double their studying time.

"I wanted to congratulate you!" His voice boomed

across the hall and part of me wanted to duck as other teachers and students turned to look.

"Congratulate me?" I asked, my voice sounding minuscule after his.

"Yes!" Geoff clapped me on the shoulder, and I stumbled sideways a pace. "I heard you were nominated for teacher of the year. As a substitute no less! I don't know what you say to these kids, but you've got them wrapped around your finger."

"I mostly just give them direction and encouragement," I murmured. My voice sounded far away to my own ears. Teacher of the year? That had to come with some kind of public attention— an icy ball of dread settled in my stomach. It almost felt as though Sarah's specter was back and the air was being sucked away from me again.

"Bah!" Geoff intoned again. "Kids don't need that much encouragement. They need a strong hand!"

"Ah," I said, dumbly, my mind spinning. "Do you know if the Dean is in his office?"

"I'd imagine so," Geoff said.

I turned to go, the students streaming past me blurred.

"Hey," Geoff's voice boomed after me. "If you aren't careful, they'll print your name in the paper every year."

I sped up my feet. That was exactly what I was afraid of.

———

"Dean Chastain will see you now," Secretary Logan said, holding the door open for me to enter.

Jill Logan had offered for me to take a seat when I had arrived and asked to see the Dean, but I had too much nervous energy in my stomach to sit still. I had paced the antechamber of the Dean's office for nearly ten minutes before the secretary waved me in. She was a kind woman. She always held a gentleness in her eyes behind her blue-framed glasses even when dealing with the most trouble-some students.

I liked her, despite the cardigan she wore buttoned up to her throat in any weather that seemed to be perpetually covered in cat hair. It wasn't that I didn't like cats. They just made my eyes water and my throat itch which was inconvenient on a good day and downright insulting on a bad one. I skirted Jill to put some distance between myself and her furry sweater and ducked into the Dean's office.

Dean Richard Chastain had overseen Crescent City Academy for longer than I had been alive. A portrait of a much younger version of the Dean graced the entryway to the main hall of the Academy, dark brown hair and brown eyes, trim build. Handsome once. Now the portrait only served to show how much time had passed since Chastain had taken charge. The man who stood as I entered the room was in his mid-sixties with white hair that was kind enough to remain attached to all of the Dean's head, and extra pounds around his middle that rose to thicken his neck and plush out his cheeks. Only those dark eyes remained the same. Smart, calculating. The eyes of a politician or a preda-tor, my father would have said. *Same difference.*

"Miss Haley," Dean Chastain held out a warm hand. "I don't believe we had an appointment today."

"No, Dean," I said, taking his hand firmly in mine. "We didn't, but I needed to meet with you unexpectedly."

"Well, please, have a seat."

Chastain gestured to a pair of plush dark leather chairs that sat before his desk. The desk too was a dark wood, as was the paneling on the walls and the shelves filled with important looking books behind his desk. It was an old sign of money, this dark wood. Imposing, almost gothic feeling. I knew this was a man who liked to feel important, but his office furniture practically *screamed* it.

The Dean settled into his high-backed leather chair. "Now, my dear. What can I do for you?"

I gritted my teeth at the use of *dear* in this context, but ignored it for the moment. I needed something from him, and I couldn't nitpick his speech and risk losing whatever good grace I had with him.

"I just heard from the master-at-arms that I was nominated for some kind of an award?"

"Indeed," Chastain's voice rumbled as he dipped his chin. "Teacher of the Year. Quite a prestigious honor, especially for a substitute teacher. You must be quite the influence on these students, Miss Haley."

"Ah, yes." I hesitated. I didn't have a very good reason for what I was about to ask him. I should have spent more time coming up with an excuse while I was pacing the office, but here I was. It was now or never. "I need to ask you to not give me this award."

The Dean opened his mouth once, then closed it. He sat back in his chair. "Now why on earth would you want to forego this honor? You are just starting out in what has the potential to be an excellent teaching career. The fact that the students love you so dearly already, is a testament to that. This award would be invaluable to you in your career moving forward."

I knew that was true. I loved this Academy and these students. I wanted to work here for a long time. That's what made it so difficult to turn this down. But I didn't have a choice. My past had taken much from me, this was the smallest of the sacrifices it demanded.

"I know this award comes with public honor and recognition and I must politely ask you to give it to someone else. I wish I could tell you more—" *lie* "—but it is very important that my name not end up in a paper somewhere and that attention stays far, far from me."

Chastain leveled me with those calculating eyes. I held his gaze.

"I know the kind of work your father does," He said finally.

I nodded.

"I know the kind of danger that he must interact with every day," Chastain reasoned slowly.

I nodded again.

"Very well. I will not pry any further. Your name will be removed from the final vote count for the award. Your students will be quite disappointed, though."

"I know."

Chastain laughed suddenly. "If I didn't know better, I'd assume you were hiding from the law, but of course we took your fingerprints when we hired you so we *know* that can't be it."

I laughed along with him, not feeling the mirth he apparently did. Dean Chastain had no idea that the fingerprints I had given him upon hire belonged to someone else. I could honestly assure him that the law enforcement of *this* city wasn't hunting me, but I had no doubt that they would hand me over to those who were without a half a second's deliberation.

"Thank you, Dean," I said, standing to leave.

"Of course, Miss Haley," he said, rising as I did. Ever the old-fashioned gentleman. "May I say, I am very pleased you are working here at the Academy. I can tell you are meant for so much more than substitute teaching."

I blinked. It was almost exactly what the spirit had told me earlier. Chastain gave me a smile that didn't reach his eyes and walked to open the door for me.

"Have a good afternoon, Dean Chastain." I said as I passed.

"Be safe, Miss Haley." His words were a warning I didn't need, and it only served to unnerve me. I waited until the door closed behind me before letting the shudder wrack my torso. Dean Chastain speaking the words of a long-dead ghost.

Eerie. It was all too eerie.

# Chapter Three

The walk from the Academy was exactly as I had expected. Despite it being the middle of the afternoon, the sun had hidden behind storm clouds all day and the rain kept most people off the streets. The smart ones huddled into cafes or streetcars to avoid the downpour. My leather jacket and umbrella kept most of it off my skin, but the late summer humidity dampened my clothing anyway. I should have worn something lighter. The urge to veer off course and find a lake or bayou to dive into hit me strong.

The encounter with Sarah and the words we exchanged seemed to have put a beacon on my head. Every specter who would have normally stayed away, wandering listlessly through the city, now seemed to find their way into my path. They didn't know why they were drawn to me. Not well enough to try to engage me in conversation. A wide-eyed specter with matted blond hair almost made eye contact with me before passing on up the street. A darker skinned man, the side of his head split by a sharp gash, cast his eyes to the right and left as he tried to find me.

A pang hit my chest at the need I saw before me. I couldn't help them. I couldn't give them peace if I tried.

I steeled myself against their searching eyes. Most of the newly dead, I could ignore. Those who were not yet powerful enough to turn physical. But the chill they left as they floated through me was enough to put me in a bad mood.

I couldn't let this continue. I had to shake them off.

Turning from the route that would have taken me home, I soon found myself treading the familiar sidewalk that led to the Agency.

My Agency.

I shuddered at the thought. What had Dad been thinking, leaving it to me after all these years?

The sign above the door read *Collier Investigations*. Underneath, the words burned into the wood in a swooping cursive was *Madame LaMontagne's Readings*. The wooden frame and lettering were darkened by the water that had pelted it all day making the words hard to discern. We should have painted them white.

The windows to the left of the door were dark and uninviting. No lights on the side of the building where my father had worked tirelessly for the last twenty years. To the right of the door, the windows were covered from the inside by dark red fabric, the flickering lights behind that casting an ominous red glow onto the street. Exactly the kind of vibe my aunt leaned into.

The front door was unlocked and the bell that father had installed years ago jingled happily as I walked in.

"Tante Flora?" I called out, warning her that it was just me approaching.

There were chairs lining the hall that split the Agency between her parlor and my father's office. The doorway to my right was draped dramatically in curtains of dark maroon and purple. Gold embroidery lined their edges. The spicy scent of incense wafted into the hall. If nothing else, my aunt liked to make dramatic first impressions.

"In the kitchen, dear." My aunt's voice came, slightly muffled by the heavy drapery.

I walked past her parlor entrance and twisted the knob on a non-descript door near the end of the hall. If you hadn't known it was there, across from the bathrooms, you might have missed it completely, which was the whole point.

Florentina LaMontagne sat at the small round table that took up the majority of the kitchen's floor space. She had lit a squat round candle and the scent of sandalwood filled the air, carried on curling whisps of smoke. The delicate teacup and saucer before her were painted with intricate blue flowers, a pattern that matched my aunt's headwrap today. Her dark lined face and light brown eyes were exactly what I had been looking for and I nearly collapsed into the chair across from her.

"Long day, dear?"

I peeled off my leather jacket and shook out the t-shirt I wore beneath it, trying to unstick it from my skin.

"Not long. Just draining."

"Tea?" The white bangles on Florentina's arms clinked against one another as she gestured toward the pot on the stove.

I shook my head, but then realized just how thirsty I really was from the walk here and got up to pour myself a glass of water.

When I sat down once more, Florentina spoke again. "Something followed you here."

The words would have sent a chill through anyone else,

but I knew what waited for me outside. I took a sip of water, cherishing the coolness of it.

"More than one something," I said.

"You spoke to one of them." It wasn't a question.

I swallowed hard. The memory of Sarah's touch flew through my mind, chilling my core. Suddenly, the tea didn't sound so bad.

"What happened to your 'ignore them and hope they go away' plan?" Her words had a bite to them. Sarcasm that stung. I'd learned that particular skill from her.

I shrugged, suddenly feeling like a small child again, chastised for poor school grades.

The bracelets sounded again as Florentina waved a hand. "It doesn't matter. They are gone."

"Thank-you, Tante."

"You are a silly girl," Florentina said. I knew the lecture that would come next. We'd been through this many times. Perhaps the only point of contention between my aunt and my father was this very subject. I fought against the deep sigh that rose in my chest. I'd come here looking for help and she'd delivered. Time to pay the piper.

"You shouldn't be ignoring them," my aunt said. I watched the light from the candle as it flickered off the gold hoops in her earlobes.

"You are one of the few in this entire city who can help those unfortunate souls, and you squander it."

I took another sip of my water. It would do no good to interrupt her now. Tante Flora was on her soapbox. The best thing to do was wait it out.

"Your father raised you to be selfish."

Her words were biting, but I couldn't argue with them. Selfishness is what had kept me hidden all these years. Self-ishness kept us alive.

"Pah!" Florentina said. "That is why you wish to sell this place. It could be your best chance to help people, but you want to throw it away."

"I help people now, Tante." I said softly, my only attempt to turn away the tide I could feel rising.

"You teach spoiled kids to succeed in a world that will only spoil them further. You teach humans who do not care for those who are different from them. They don't even value *magic*. They have only their fear of the other, and they would stamp out anything that they don't understand as though it were a threat." Florentina's face seemed to darken further as she aired her anger. The candle flame grew, a pillar of heat that threatened the small table. The lightbulbs in the ceiling seemed to dim, sending longer lines around her face. A harsh breeze swirled the table, picking at the strands of hair that had escaped my ponytail and throwing them into my face.

This was Madame LaMontagne. The most powerful magic practitioner in the city. She whose name thrust fear into the hearts of those who would seek to wrong her. Whose clients even held her at a safe and respectful distance.

My aunt.

I kept my voice level. The Madame didn't scare me. She should, but she didn't.

What can I say, I've never claimed to be wise.

"I'm in a position to teach those children to be more tolerant," I said. "To understand that there are lives beyond Mansion Row and there are other children who need their help. I am in a place where I can shape a generation to not fear magic, to not hide from it, but to embrace it. To use it. That is why I am at the Academy."

My aunt stared at me for a long moment. The flame of

the candle returned to its normal height. The wind died down enough that I could smooth the hair back from my face.

Florentina picked up her teacup and saucer and took a delicate sip.

"You don't need to sell the Agency," she said finally. "You can do good here, also."

I clenched my jaw until it ached. I couldn't argue with her logic. I had the time between teaching gigs to work cases, but still a part of me pushed against returning to this life. Returning to the running and chasing and fighting that came with it.

"I never wanted this," my voice was a whisper. "Dad knew that. Why would he leave it to me?"

Aunt Flora's teacup clinked as she set it back onto the table. "You could always ask him."

An unexpected huffing noise escaped me. After the last argument we exchanged, I'm sure I was the *last* person my father wanted to hear from.

The colorful strings of bead around Florentina's neck rustled as she rose. A familiar tinkling that had been the melody of my childhood. Her wide white skirts pushed the chair back from behind her. "I have a four thirty reading I must prepare for."

I hesitated. Even with the ghosts gone, I wasn't quite ready to head home. "Do you know, did Dad have any outstanding cases before he left?"

My aunt set her teacup and saucer in the sink and filled them with water. "I don't believe so, dear. There have been reports of a kid missing off Bourbon Street..."

I grimaced. I hated missing kids. In all the years I had assisted my father in his investigations, I had never gotten used to the kid cases. They never ended well.

"I think we'll let the cops handle that one."

Florentina let out a delicate snort and swept out of the room through the curtained doorway that led directly to her parlor.

I wandered back out to the hallway. Someone, either my father or aunt had hung paintings on the walls of the otherwise drab waiting area. A streetcar passing through the French Quarter, a steamboat on the Mississippi. They were beautiful. Must have been Tante's touch.

I came to a stop before Dad's office door. The frosted glass window said everything it needed to assure clients they were in the right place.

David Collier
Private Investigator
Paranormal and Other

I took a deep breath. It had been years since I'd been inside this office. Years since I had told Dad I was taking the job at Crescent City Academy. I had visited the Agency since then, sure. Mostly to see Tante Flora and the occasional dinner upstairs in Dad's apartment, but I hadn't entered his office since working side by side with him on cases.

"The door isn't going to open itself." My aunt's voice shook me from my memories. I turned, expecting to see her standing in the doorway to her parlor, but the heavy curtains across the hall were still closed.

I shook my head and turned the knob, taking another breath to steel myself before entering the office.

It was almost exactly as I remembered it. Dad's desk sat directly before me, two plush chairs facing it and one swivel chair behind. On the desk sat an upright computer that was practically ancient, but Dad always swore it worked perfectly fine, thank you very much. A short bookcase sat below the windowsill. I ran my fingers over the familiar spines. Old detective novels lined the top shelves, with legal texts and science related subjects underneath. Dad had been a scientist first, before hiding me drove him to this city and he had to give up his first love. Well, not entirely.

I looked to the doors across from the window. Any visitor to this office would assume they led to a coat closet, but I knew behind those double doors was his entire laboratory. Dad never trusted the city crime lab, not after NOPD had destroyed almost all evidence they had gotten their hands on from absolute paranormal ignorance. The police department had since learned that you couldn't store magical artifacts alongside physical evidence, but Dad had always said that he didn't trust them as far as he could throw them. So, anything he picked up in his investigations came back here, for his personal experimentations.

I sat in the swivel chair behind the desk and booted up the computer. A leafy plant sat in a pot beside the monitor, and I felt its leaves. Plastic, thank goodness. Leaving me the Agency was one thing, but I couldn't be responsible to keep plant life alive. Part of me wondered if Dad had remembered the middle school chlorophyll study I had done that resulted in the deaths of more tiny plants than I could count and a frankly ridiculous amount of frustrated tears on both our parts.

I smiled slightly. There were good memories. Plenty of them, in fact. My gaze drifted to the framed photo beside the plant. My eyes stung at the sight of it. It was from my graduation when I had received my teaching credentials.

I was wearing the most outrageously gaudy yellow gown that made my complexion look sickly. A lock of brown hair that Tante Flora had curled for me was poking me in the eye, but Dad was grinning beside me. For once, he had shaved the scruffy shadow he usually sported and the grin he wore showed off all of the smile lines he had collected over the years. His gray eyes shone in the flash of the photographer's camera.

I felt a hitch in my throat. He hated that I left the Agency to pursue that degree but damn if he hadn't cheered louder than any other parent in the audience that graduation day. I could almost hear the words he whispered to me just before the photographer snapped the picture. "I'm always proud of you, Meranda. No matter what."

I pressed the heels of my hands into my eyes.

Damn it, Dad. Then why did you leave?

# Chapter Four

"The Agency is completely in the red." I twisted the mug of coffee in my hands, watching the milk swirl through the dark liquid. "It seems like Dad has been bankrupt for years."

Brigitte le Blanc cut open the cardboard box that I had set on her kitchen table with one deft stroke of a scalpel. I found the package on her front porch as I walked up, and it was habit that made me pick it up and bring it inside. It was no surprise to me that my best friend found it simpler to use a scalpel to carve open the thing than to search her kitchen for a pair of scissors. Having known each other for over a decade, not much about us surprised one another. It was an understanding friendship that made me walk to her house as soon as I had finished perusing the files Dad had left on his desktop.

Brigitte's tawny hair was bound up in a green bandanna today, causing the mass of it to stick up from the crown of her head like a bird-of-paradise and tiny rogue locks to coil beside her ears. Her light brown skin had been given to her by some ancestor who had come from Jamaica, but her father had left her with blue-green eyes that sparkled in the sun and a subtle smattering of freckles that graced her nose and cheeks. I had grown up staring into that face more times than I could count as we shared secrets with one other as children, both of us living among humans from whom we had something to hide.

"Your dad always liked to help people," Brigitte said softly. "Even when they couldn't afford it."

I rubbed my eyes. I knew that. It was that same bleeding heart toward the lost that saved my life twenty-seven years ago.

"It just feels like adding insult to injury to leave me the Agency *and* leave the finances in such disarray that I can't just sell the thing."

"Maybe he didn't want you to sell it," Brigitte murmured. She pulled a vacuum sealed package out of the confines of the box and turned it over in her hands. A cloudy liquid surrounded some kind of greyish-pink tissue within.

"The hell kind of gruesome novelty is that?" I asked, burying my nose into my coffee cup in case the horror also carried a smell with it.

"It's a fetal pig," Brigitte said, matter-of-factly. "Didn't you take high school biology?"

"Well, sure, but by the time it got to me, it wasn't floating in nasty hotdog water."

Brigitte made a face. "You really make the strangest comparisons."

I shrugged. "What can I say, it's a gift. Is this a surprise for the children of Crescent City's finest next week?"

"It will be a couple of weeks before we get to actually dissect it. I ordered most of the supplies early this year. Trade routes in and out of the city are delayed from all the

—" she searched for the right word, "—preparations that are being made."

I'd seen signs of those preparations all over the city in the last few weeks. There was restlessness in the Gulf. It made the Council nervous. Mer-Checks were being instituted all across the city and at all major public venues. It was a ridiculous measure. Any sufficiently powerful melusine could withstand their simple saline checks with little discomfort. Despite their ineffectiveness, the checks made the Council feel as though they were doing *something* to protect the people who had elected them. Mostly, it just delayed travel and shipments coming to and from New Orleans.

The price of the illusion of safety, I supposed.

Brigitte returned the clear plastic pack to the box and pushed it aside. "Well, what are you going to do?"

I scratched a thumbnail across the handle of the worn coffee mug. I'd given this set to Brigitte when she'd first taken the biology teaching job at Crescent City Academy. One of the mugs made reference to the tears of biology students, another had two strands of DNA with one complaining 'stop copying me'. They had made me laugh. Brigitte had offered a long-suffering smile when she'd unwrapped them, but each time I came to visit, these were what we drank from.

"I had hoped to give it to Samuel. He's been working with Dad these last couple of years since I—left."

Brigitte made a non-committal humming noise.

"I don't know." I sipped my coffee again. "I can't saddle him with this kind of debt. It wouldn't be right. And you *know* I don't make enough substituting to bring it to a manageable level."

"You could keep it." Brigitte must have seen the face

I made as she rapidly backpedaled. "Just for a little while. Work a couple of cases, ones that actually pay well. You were always so good at the cases when your dad needed you. Then sell it or give it to Samuel or whatever. I know you kept your P.I. license active. It's not like anything is stopping you from picking it right back up."

I grimaced. It's not that I didn't enjoy the work or helping people. It's just—every case seemed to come with supernatural troubles. I was out of practice defending against the paranormal entities that I'd encounter. The last time I spoke to a spirit on a case hadn't ended well. I blinked hard to wipe the image of bloodstains and claw marks from my mind.

"Dad didn't have any outstanding cases. I'm not really looking to put my name out there and advertise for them. No one in this city knows who I am anyway. Why would they trust no-name Meranda Haley with their investigatory needs?"

"You don't have to use your name," Brigitte said, patience gracing her tone. I didn't deserve that. I was complaining. "You'll be working out of your dad's office. David Collier's name still carries weight. Operate under that. Anyone would believe that he's too busy with other cases to talk to witnesses himself. Of course he'd have a liaison for that."

I couldn't argue with that. Plenty of P.I.s in the city used teams to do their investigating. No one who hired me would think it was strange if they didn't actually *see* the Collier behind Collier Investigations.

"You always have to be right, don't you?" I asked.

My best friend smiled. "What can I say, it's a gift. Now can I *please* do something about the tension around you. It's like the whole room is a bristle pad rubbing you the wrong way."

I held up a hand. "Fine. But only if you're very gentle. It's been a long week."

Brigitte rose to stand behind my chair. "Come on, when am I *not* gentle with you?"

I swallowed the list seventeen years in the making that immediately threatened to answer that challenge. I pushed my shoulders back and dropped them low, preparing the canvas for her deft hands.

Her warm hands dropped to my shoulders, and I got a whiff of the coconut from her hand lotion. I closed my eyes against the soft glow that began to emit from her palms. A rush of air escaped my lips as Brigitte ran her hands over my shoulders and upper arms. Her palms weren't directly against me, now, but hovered a little away from my shirt, allowing the yellow glowing light to bathe my arms.

When I opened my eyes again, the room seemed clearer, my head felt lighter. It was almost as though the stresses of life, while I could still remember them, weren't quite so pressing on my mind.

"Thank you," I breathed.

"Happy to help," Brigitte said, brushing her hands together as though shaking water from them.

She took her seat again across from me and picked up her coffee. "I know you're not convinced yet, but I can tell you, there are plenty in this city who could use a good investigator. Heavens knows half the residents of this city can't trust the police department for help."

"I know," I said. "I'll think about it. Promise."

Suddenly her eyes sparkled in the kitchen lights. "Good. Now let's check the porch again, I'm expecting some desiccated sea stars for the next unit's dissections."

I grimaced. "Awesome."

---

I sat outside of the Dean's office feeling like nothing so much as a scolded school child awaiting punishment. The only sounds were the hum of the air conditioner, fighting valiantly to keep the humid August weather *outside* these walls, and the clacking of Secretary Logan's acrylic nails on her keyboard.

A student, on loan to the Dean, had found me as I left my last class. The quickly relayed message gave no detail as to what the Dean wanted to talk to me about, only that I needed to stop by his office at my 'earliest convenience'. It was another old-timey phrase. It meant *now*.

As I stared at the toes of my short brown boots, barely visible beneath the flared tan dress pants that I wore, I couldn't help but think through the myriad of reasons I could have been called here. Very few of them were good. I spent much of the previous evening re-warding the grounds of the Academy, but I didn't think the Dean would know that.

Whatever magic Florentina had worked yesterday had kept the ghosts at bay throughout the night. I was left undisturbed as I dug trenches and laid rock salt and buried the lines again. It wasn't the most ideal method to regulate the spirits' movement as the rains tended to wear down the defenses over time, but it offered some reprieve until I could get a more permanent fix. Perhaps I could find a priest who still had enough faith in the old religions who would be willing to bless the grounds. Those faithful priests were getting harder and harder to find these days.

The horrors that had emerged from the portals were

enough to shake anyone's faith. There was a considerable lack of parishioners left when churches reopened their doors. Most priests had to move on to other careers. I had heard of a booming exorcism industry up north, but New Orleans faithful were hard to find. Maybe Father Jeremiah was still around. I could call him. It had been years, but—

A chime sounded from the phone beside the secretary, and she picked it up without taking her eyes off the screen in front of her. A few seconds and one 'yes sir' later, and Logan looked up at me.

"Dean Chastain will see you now."

I stood and thanked her. The dark wooden doors to Dean Chastain's office were heavier than they looked. I let out an unexpected 'oof' as I pushed them open. It occurred to me then, that Secretary Logan probably had more muscle on her than those skinny cardigans let on.

"Ah, Miss Haley." Dean Chastain rose from behind his desk as I entered. "Please, come have a seat."

A sinking feeling sent my stomach down somewhere deep in my gut. Again, the thought of being a chastised child flew through my mind. I squared my shoulders. It was this office. It was the time the Dean had put into designing it to intimidate students who actually *had* done something worth the headmaster's punishment. I had done plenty wrong by this city's standards, but none of it was the job of the Dean to punish. I forced myself to take slow sure steps across the plush carpet and settled delicately onto the seat of one of the dark leather chairs that faced his desk.

"I'm sure you've heard that a young woman was kidnapped off Bourbon Street this last week." Dean Chastain said as he took his seat again.

No 'How are you?' or even 'I bet you're wondering why

I called you in here'. Straight to business. This didn't feel like a normal meeting in the Dean's office.

"You called me in here to talk about headlines?" I asked. When surprised by a question, it was often best to respond with a question of your own.

"The child who was taken is a student of this institution." The Dean's voice held no trace of humor. It wouldn't. This involved someone under his charge.

"I'm sorry, I didn't know," I said, truthfully.

"The Bettencourt family has been a major donor to this academy for decades. We have schooled four of their children to graduation and Lucy was to be our final success for them."

He paused as though for me to congratulate him. I waited. He hadn't asked a question.

"The Bettencourts reached out to your father for help."

Ah, that was why I had been called in here.

"My father is out of town. He didn't say when he would be back," I explained. The lie was easy to tell. Far easier than the truth.

"I am not a subtle man, Miss Haley. I had hoped to call you in here to appeal to your understanding nature, to convince you of the gravity of the situation."

I waited again. Again, he hadn't asked a question.

"I will make this as plain as possible. It would be a detriment to this Academy, and to your future career if this family does not receive their little girl back — unharmed."

I felt his words like a jab. "Are you threatening my job, Dean?"

"I do not make threats, Miss Haley," the Dean said. "But my word holds weight with every major institution in this city. It would be a shame if a teacher of your talent couldn't get work."

I don't make threats, my ass.

"I understand what you're saying, but I have told you, my father is out of town. He is not even *here* to investigate this case."

"You are his daughter, are you not?"

That was complicated.

"You hold sway in his decisions."

That was less complicated. I nodded.

Dean Chastain held up his hands, an open gesture as though I had just confirmed whatever he was trying to say.

"Will that be all?" I asked, consciously keeping myself from gritting my teeth.

"Yes, Miss Haley. That will be all."

# Chapter Five

The walk home from the Academy felt longer than usual. The sky had clouded over and rains threatened, but none had fallen yet this day. Instead, a cloying humidity stuck to everything I passed. Old iron fence-work and light-poles wept with amassed moisture. The heaviness of the air clung to my hair and limbs, weighing me down. Or maybe it was the gravity of the ultimatum I'd been offered.

I knew Dean Chastain held sway over every school in New Orleans. I knew he hadn't been bluffing when he'd told me I may never teach again if I didn't do this for him. Or for the Bettencourt family. Whatever.

I didn't like that he had that kind of power over me. If I agreed to help, or told him that I had convinced my *dad* to help, he'd know that he could get anything out of me. There was no freedom in that.

It wasn't just about the kid who was taken. It was about being a slave to this man's wishes. This *human*. His old-fashioned southern politeness could very easily be a facade. I didn't trust that it would hold when he didn't get his way.

But then, the Dean was right: if I ever wanted to teach, to offer some *balance* in the minds of the children of this city, I had to take the job. Brigitte's words offered some silver lining also. Maybe this case would be enough to pay off the Agency's debts. Maybe I'd be free of it at the end of all of this.

My walk brought me closer to the waterfront. The Mississippi River was swollen with the recent rains and muddied enough that I couldn't see to the bottom. A part of me longed for the clear blue of the waters of the Caribbean, but it had been a long time since I'd visited those. Still the water rushing beside me calmed me as I walked. The sound of water always did.

A cry ahead of me drew my attention. Any thoughts of my own day's woes vanished as I saw the commotion taking place twenty feet up the river from where I walked.

"A body!" the cry came. "A body in the water!"

The sound of someone diving from the riverbank into the Mississippi reached my ears.

I broke into a sprint.

Other passersby had been drawn by the cries and I arrived on the scene to find a small crowd forming already. I shoved my way through the gathering throng and threw myself to the ground beside the bank. Two other men joined me, and we thrust our hands down toward the water trying to catch hold of the man who had dived in.

His dark hair was plastered to his forehead, and he coughed and spluttered as he struggled to reach us and still maintain his hold on the crumpled form in his arms.

"Pass it to us!" I yelled, gesturing toward the bundle he held.

The man strained to extend the cloth covered weight. I

managed to snag ahold of part of the dark cloth. A sleeve, I realized. An arm inside of it. Shit. It really was a body.

The man to my right helped me haul the body onto the bank and I rolled it onto its back. Long hair obscured the pale face and dark clothing covered a torso that ended too soon. I stand corrected; it was half a body.

I pushed the hair aside and jerked my hand back. The man beside me turned away and gagged. The victim's face, for certainly it was a victim, was bloated from its time in the river. Cheeks puffed out and pale, looking as though they would burst at a touch. The lips would have been swollen too if they had still been attached. They hung on by scraps of flesh and I stared down at the ghoulish grin, the exposed teeth. Gaping nostrils were all that remained where a nose should have been. The eye sockets were empty. The lids nothing more than shredded bits of flesh. I knew what had done this.

The name of the creature made its way through the crowd, a sound of horror passing through the mass.

*Rusalka.*

A dripping form hit the ground beside me as the man who had dived in after the body finally made it to land. He coughed and spluttered, but I couldn't tear my eyes away from the form before us.

It wasn't just the legs that were missing. One arm had been torn away also. I was sure it was long gone by now. The flesh in the stomach of the unreasoning beast who had done this. It didn't make a whole hell of a lot of sense, the way rusalki left their victims.

You'd think a hungry creature would attack the abdomen and organs of their prey. That kind of meat would sustain you for a while. But not rusalki. Their reason had left them when they were banished from the melusines' home. Swimming up the rivers and bayous and leaving behind the salt of the Gulf, they had lost the only part of them that could be even remotely recognized as human.

Now, they attacked without mercy. Not only for food, but for the pleasure of killing. For the joy of seeing the fear on their victim's face before they stripped it down to bone. It was the fear they craved. The stress hormones pumping through their victim's body that made the flesh taste so good. I had seen even well-fed rusalki treat a human victim with the same gleeful violence. Rusalka attacks weren't especially common this close to the Gulf, but damn were they memorable.

There was a reason the humans of this city feared the melusine, the half fish, half humans who resided in the Gulf. But I knew, this close to the city, there was far more danger in the rusalka. They couldn't leave the water, but they were patient, opportunistic hunters. An unsuspecting human wandering into the water was easy prey. The humans didn't care to differentiate between the two. Danger from rusalki meant danger from anything that looked like them, whether they could be reasoned with or not.

Sirens sounded, growing closer. Someone had called the police.

I pushed to my feet, finally turning away from the sight. This was just perfect. A rusalka attack this close to the city. The humans would be insufferable for weeks. Forget mer-checks, it wouldn't surprise me if they shut the whole city down.

I slipped away before anyone could stop me. Before anyone could ask me questions. I didn't have any answers they'd want to hear.

Scared humans didn't want the truth.

It was only a short way to my neighborhood from the river. The familiar winding streets felt solid beneath my feet, grounding me even as my arms and face were numbed.

My feet came to a halt before the tall iron gates of my fenced-in community. When I first left the apartment above the Agency, striking out on my own, all I could have afforded resided in run down neighborhoods near the jankiest parts of the city. David Collier would never allow it. We'd compromised when he'd offered to cover the down payment for a house no one wanted in a protected community. Due to the details that made this house a veritable pariah on its well-paved street, I got a steal on the mortgage. I'd been fortunate enough to have steady substituting jobs that kept my expenses in the black.

The house ghost hardly bothered me anyway.

"Meeess Haley," the exaggerated drawl caught my attention, and I turned as the lanky guard unfolded himself from the small security booth beside the front gate.

"Joseph," I greeted him. "A good day so far?"

Joseph Bernard had been the security guard for my neighborhood since long before I had moved in. He always wore his gray button up starched and pressed with his Arnold Securities patch well displayed on his left shoulder. His hat with a matching patch was often askew as he had a habit of pushing his greasy brown bangs back from his face throughout the day. I would have opted for a haircut, myself, but he seemed attached to his tic, so I didn't bring it up.

"A good day, Meeess Haley," Joseph agreed. "Very good. Fine fishin' weather comin' in."

I nodded. Joseph didn't seem to acknowledge that bad

fishing weather was even possible. Any day off, it seemed, he was in one of the bayous. I'd seen him at times when I walked near the water. He had a worn wooden rowboat he used as he cast his line and he would be out there for hours humming to himself. *Simple pleasures*, I thought. *A good life.*

"You watch yourself out on those bayous," I said. "The city is getting awfully jumpy about what lives out there."

Joseph made an exasperated noise and pushed at his bangs, tilting his hat farther back on his head. "I've fished on them bayous my whole life, Meeess. I ain't never been bothered by no gators or them rusalki neither. But if it makes you feel better, I always got somethin' to defend myself anyways."

"Good man, Joseph," I said.

"I heard your papa was outta town on business?" It sounded like a question.

"Yeah, he didn't say exactly where he was going," I lied. "I don't know when he'll be back."

"Oh." The toe of Joseph's boot scuffed the line of dirt between two cobble stones. "Well, when he gets back, wouldja tell him I'd like to speak with him."

"Sure," I said. Joseph had been after my father for a job for years. As long as I'd known him, Joseph had believed he would do more good somewhere bigger than this small security box. I didn't have the heart to tell him that he didn't have a chance. That my father wouldn't be giving out jobs anytime in the near future.

Joseph stepped up to the gate and pushed the smaller pedestrian door open.

"Have a good day, Meeess Haley," he said as I passed through.

"You too. Don't get too bored out here."

"Naw." Joseph let out a small chuckle. "I've got my shows. No boredom here."

Joseph made his way back to his small booth and the six inch beat up T.V. that I knew awaited him. *Simple pleasures,* I thought again. Maybe Joseph had it right. He sure seemed happier than most of the people I passed on the street who could probably afford far more than a rowboat and an old television.

I walked the well-kept street that led to my modest house. It was the smallest structure in the row, as if it had been built before people decided that your worth could be quantified by the square footage you owned. The roof had held up to the rain well through the three years I'd lived here, even though my dad had threatened to replace it each summer. It occurred to me that he hadn't lodged those threats this last year. He probably wouldn't get a chance to again.

I bit the inside of my cheek against the stinging in my eyes. I felt the ward I passed through to enter my home. Florentina had insisted on it when I moved out of my dad's apartment. She had talked to whatever entity hung onto the old house and dismissed it as a non-threat before warding the outside of the structure within an inch of its life. The ward was designed to keep out unwanted supernatural visitors, but I realized that meant my house guest was trapped inside with me without a hope of escape. We'd found a steady rhythm over the years, and we didn't bother one another too much. Actually, if you asked *her, I* was the strange house guest who wouldn't leave.

"It's me," I called as I kicked my shoes off in the narrow entryway. A flash of movement out of the corner of my eye and a small cold hand brushing against my own was the only acknowledgment of my arrival.

Marie Breton had been trapped in this home since her death almost a decade ago. Her less than welcoming attitude towards newcomers had kept this home empty long enough for me to find it. At first, I hadn't wanted anything to do with the place. I had been fresh off one of the worst supernatural experiences of my life. A case that had been twisted six ways from Sunday. A few stern words from Florentina had convinced Marie to give me a chance and reluctantly, I'd agreed to move in.

Now, this had become my home. A strange, shared establishment. I didn't bother Marie about her past, and she didn't bother me about my present. It was rare for her to show herself or speak to me, too much effort for such a young spirit, I assumed. The few times she had spoken, her voice sounded young. Impossibly young to have passed on peacefully, which explained her inability to move on and settle.

A cool breeze ran across the floorboards and a letter skittered to a stop at my feet. I picked it up. No return address, but in large sweeping cursive I could read who it had been sent to: Marie Breton.

"Do you want to read it?" I asked into the empty room.

A small glass lamp on an end table in the living room blinked on.

"Okay," I whispered.

I opened the letter with a sharp knife I kept hidden behind the mirror in my entryway. The house was warded against supernatural visitors, but a young woman living alone could never be too careful. I took the tri-folded pieces of paper out without reading them and set them open on the end table. The light from the lamp illuminated the handwritten script.

I retreated to the kitchen to give Marie some privacy. I

poured myself some iced tea from the fridge and shook a few dashes of lemon juice from a bottle into it. I was just sitting down in my chair when a short gust sent the top page of the letter fluttering to the floor as Marie read on.

This wasn't the first letter she'd received. I'd never read them, respecting her privacy too much for that, but I could feel her mood change after each one. It wasn't that she was angry or depressed afterward. It was a strange melancholy that filled our home. Whoever it was that wrote to her. She missed them.

I lit the candle that sat in the middle of the kitchen table, a cheerful blend of honey and lavender. It wouldn't be enough to dispel Marie's coming mood, I knew, but I liked to think it would help. I left the candle burning as I made my way down the hall to my bedroom. Before I closed the door, I heard a soft sob from the living room.

I let out a sigh that I hoped would ease some of the ache from my chest and leaned back against the door.

The grief in that small sobbing noise was enough to squeeze my heart. It was at that moment that it became clear to me. There was another family in this city whose hearts were weighed down with grief. Well, I'm sure there were plenty, but there was one in particular whom I could help. The Bettencourt's pain was fresh, and it was something I could actually *do* something about. I couldn't find the motivation to help them because of Chastain's threats or the debts against the Agency. It was that agony that I knew they were feeling with their little girl missing. That was why I had to help.

I knew what I had to do.

I had to take the case.

# Chapter Six

The Bettencourt home wanted very desperately to look like the governor's mansion, but just barely fell short. Still, it was an imposing sight to behold. White painted, covered in windows, three stories tall. The wrap-around porch with its wrought-iron railing matched the soaring balconies above. Imposing white pillars were strategically spaced between the French windows so as to not obscure the view of the sprawling lawn from inside the residence . The scent of fresh cut grass greeted me, earthy in the heat of the day.

I had called the Dean's secretary shortly after my decision to take the case and she was prepared with all the contact information for the Bettencourt family. It was almost as though she'd had it ready for me, just waiting for my call. I tried not to let that bother me.

My soft leather boots ground into the graveled drive as I made my way toward the front steps. I hadn't bothered to change before taking the streetcar to the intersection nearest Mansion Row and walking from there. The tan slacks and cream blouse were light enough for the August heat and my short boots offered enough support that my feet didn't complain about the trek.

I knew from the years I had worked alongside my father that most clients felt at ease when the investigator they met with dressed business casual. They didn't want to see the nitty gritty of really functional clothes for chasing bad guys. Especially here on Mansion Row. Dark leathers and combat boots made people nervous.

A bell sounded somewhere deep in the house when I pressed the button beside the tall windowed front door. A few quick steps clacked on what I assumed was a well-polished marble floor, and the door swung open before me. The slight figure who answered the door blinked at me with large blue eyes.

"May I help you?"

Her skin was a pale blue, appearing washed out and dull in the strictly-tailored, white, maid's uniform. Light brown hair pulled into a tight bun behind her head, only served to accent the pointed tips to her ears. A lower fae, one of the many creatures who had been forced by the humans of the city into the impossible choice between menial work and criminality.

"I am a liaison from Collier Investigations," I said, offering a smile that would put her at ease. "I believe Ms. Bettencourt is expecting me."

"Yes, Miss," the fae took a step back while inclining her head. "Please follow me."

As we walked through the home, I took in the meticulously curated decor. Bright white paint on the walls and pillars, white marble floors—the green of vines and potted plants were the only splash of color in the place, leaving me with a cool distant feeling. I noted only one family portrait. It hung in the hallway that the fae led me down. Not the most prominent position in the home, but it was an impressive painting, nonetheless. The Bettencourt parents were front and center, seated on a low couch, their older children, three boys and a girl, standing solemn around them. And there, on Mrs. Bettencourt's lap, a slight girl with large eyes and soft brown curls framing her face. Lucy Bettencourt.

She had to have been closer to four or five years old when the portrait was painted. Judging the age difference between she and her older siblings, I'd imagine they were all in their mid to late twenties now as Lucy finished high school.

"The older Bettencourt children," I asked the maid as we walked. "Are they in town, helping their parents now?"

The fae shook her head without looking at me. "The males are at the Academy in Atlanta and the female left for Texas a few years ago."

The maid lowered her tone. "The Bettencourts do not speak to her."

Ah. I knew Texas was a sore spot for many of the well-established families in New Orleans, with the military running the cities, and mercenaries and rangers being the primary export. To not speak to your daughter after she left... I couldn't imagine my father doing that to me.

Robert and Louisa Bettencourt were taking tea in the parlor when I arrived. They sat beside one another on a pale pink chaise lounge. Before them was a tea service laid out on a low dark wood table.

Robert Bettencourt wore his wealth like a well-fitted suit. From the expensive looking haircut that left a few streaks of gray at his temples to the gold watch on his right wrist, he was the picture of confident investment. A gray vest and slacks clothed his trim frame. The sleeves of his white dress shirt were rolled up, the only indication that he was relaxing and not about to pitch an idea to a boardroom full of investors.

Louisa Bettencourt was a more muted picture. I knew her white blouse was made from an expensive cut of cloth, but it didn't stand out and shout its cost. Fine lines around her eyes and lips were softened by a dusting of foundation. Her short brown hair was swept casually out of her face to be secured by unseen hairpins. She had a quiet sort of heaviness about her. It pulled at the edges of her mouth, strained the corners of her eyes. She was a grieving mother in a society that expected perfection from their elites. I couldn't imagine the kind of pressure she was under.

A small gasp left Louisa's lips when the maid and I entered the room and her teacup clattered back to its saucer as she set it down. I couldn't help but feel that my arrival interrupted some kind of tense silence between the two Bettencourts.

"Ms. Haley," she said, pulling herself together the way one would pull a shawl around themselves. "I hadn't expected you so soon."

Mr. Bettencourt offered me a firm handshake before resuming his seat and gesturing me into a white settee across the low table from them.

"Yes, well, time is of the essence in these types of cases."

At my words, Mrs. Bettencourt let out a small wail and pressed a handkerchief to her mouth. I gave her a sympathetic look but didn't change my words. They had to know that I understood the gravity of the case before me.

Mr. Bettencourt cleared his throat once. "We had—uh—hoped that Mr. Collier would be here."

I read the question in his voice. I had prepared for it. "Mr. Collier is out of town on another case." The words came easily after having said them so often. "But I assure you, he will be apprised of every detail of this case." I crossed one knee over the other as I settled into the couch.

"We had read that David Collier was the best at—this sort of thing." Mrs. Bettencourt's voice choked. "I'd feel better if he was here."

"Now, dear." Mr. Bettencourt's placating voice rubbed me sideways. "I'm sure it's the Collier *Agency* that is so highly recommended. It's no surprise that Mr. Collier would rely on others to do most of the leg work." As he said the word 'leg', his eyes traveled up my trousers in a way that made my skin crawl. Humans responded to grief and crisis in a myriad of unexpected ways, but leering at the private investigator you had hired to help? That was odd. I tucked it away in the back of my mind.

Louisa seemed to not notice her husband's emphasis, instead clapping her hands once. "Freda, please bring a cup for Ms. Haley. She'll be joining us for tea."

I nearly opened my mouth to assure her that there was no need, but I caught myself. This was southern hospitality. It would be rude to refuse. And more than that, this was the only thing Mrs. Bettencourt felt she *could* do. She was out of her depth, drowning in grief, but this—this she could do.

The maid, Freda, set a teacup and saucer on the table before me. I murmured my thanks and Mrs. Bettencourt's shoulders seemed to lighten as she relaxed into her role as hostess. I pulled a small notebook out of the pocket that was stitched into the thigh of my pants and clicked open the attached pen.

"I'd like to start by hearing about your daughter."

I could see Mrs. Bettencourt's throat working past the lump that I was sure was lodged there. Mr. Bettencourt looked at his wife and reached out a hand to squeeze her knee once before speaking. "Lucy was happy. The best daughter we could have asked for. She was good at school; all her friends liked her. I'm sorry, I'm not sure what you're looking for?"

"You're doing great," I assured him, noting the past tense he used when describing her. "Tell me about the day Lucy disappeared."

Mrs. Bettencourt's eyes were glued to her husband's hand on her leg. The hands clasped in her lap were almost white as they gripped each other.

"It was a normal day," Mr. Bettencourt continued. "She got home from school in the afternoon. Practiced piano for a while and asked to go out to meet her friends for the evening."

"I told her no," Mrs. Bettencourt's voice was a whisper. She looked up finally, tears standing out in her green eyes. "It was a Wednesday night. We always eat dinner together as a *family* on Wednesdays."

"It's not your fault," Mr. Bettencourt's tone was stern. "She wouldn't have been any safer if you'd given her permission."

Mrs. Bettencourt nodded once, pressing the handkerchief again to her mouth as tears leaked from her eyes. She blamed herself, that much was clear. *That* was a typical human response to this situation.

"She snuck out?" I asked, prompting them forward.

Mr. Bettencourt took a deep breath. "Yes, sometime after dinner. Maybe eight or eight thirty, she went up to her room to do homework. She was such a good student." There it was again, past tense.

"Do you have cameras on your property, Mr. Bettencourt?"

Mr. Bettencourt's cheeks reddened. "I'm working on getting them replaced."

Ah, no video of her getting into a car that evening. No clue who had picked her up from home.

"And the establishment from which she was—taken? Did you know where she was going?"

Mrs. Bettencourt spoke up then. "She had asked to meet her friends at The Rooster That must be where she went."

*Not necessarily*, I thought. "Did Lucy have a laptop or cell phone? Some kind of tech she used for school, maybe?"

"The police already searched her room." Mr. Bettencourt said. "They took everything into evidence."

I nodded. That's what I'd expected to hear. I needed to make a few phone calls.

"I would like a list of her friends, acquaintances, a boyfriend maybe, anyone who may have been with her Wednesday night."

Mrs. Bettencourt nodded and took the pad and paper I handed her, immediately working to write the list.

"I'd like to see her room."

"The police already searched it," Mr. Bettencourt said.

"If you trusted the police to handle this with no issues, would you have hired Collier Investigations?"

Mr. Bettencourt shook his head, but his lips were drawn into a thin line as though he didn't like the reminder that he needed my help.

"Freda," Mrs. Bettencourt called. "Please show Ms. Haley to Lucy's room."

The slight fae appeared within seconds of her name being spoken and inclined her head to me, the tips of her ears bobbing slightly with the motion.

I followed the maid back toward the entryway of the house and up a winding staircase. We stopped on the second floor, and the young fae led me down a hall to a door that looked like all the other doors we had passed. This house had to have a few dozen bedrooms.

"Thank you, Freda," I said as the fae pushed the door open.

"It is Freyja," the fae whispered, almost too softly for me to hear.

"Freyja," I repeated back. "How long have you worked for the Bettencourts?"

"Two years, Ma'am."

Long enough for them to learn to pronounce her name properly.

"No more Ma'am," I said. "Call me Meranda."

The side of Freyja's mouth quirked up at that.

I entered Lucy's bedroom and the maid stood in the doorway watching me. The room was a typical teenager's. Posters on the walls of bands I didn't recognize, one of which had a lead singer I could tell was a vamp: his sharp teeth and pale skin too subtle to have been make-up. Often, when humans tried to portray the children of the night, they exaggerated their appearance too far, creating caricatures.

The desk was strewn with papers and notebooks. A biology textbook lay open on the left side. Half the floor was littered with clothes and open dresser drawers showed where they'd come from. It could have been a product of the police department's search, but I remembered what it was like to get dressed for a night out with friends. The number of clothing items thrown across the floor and bed were small potatoes compared to the chaos I used to leave behind.

I walked to the window of the bedroom and looked out. At least twenty feet to the lawn below.

"How would Lucy have left Wednesday?"

Freyja was at my side in an instant. Fae speed. She

pushed the window open, the panes swinging out and pointed beneath it to the left of the window. A trellis. Vines ran up and down its length, but I could see plenty of exposed beams that would have made excellent foot and hand holds.

"Ah," I said.

Freyja nodded beside me. "Indeed. Ahhh!" She didn't raise her voice, but I could tell she was mimicking a scream.

I got the impression that this fae didn't like heights.

I turned back to face the room and gave it another quick once over. The police had taken anything of interest, I was sure.

Freyja led me back down the stairs and into the parlor. Mr. Bettencourt was no longer in the room, but Mrs. Bettencourt had finished the list, and I took it from her outstretched hand. "I added a few of the places she often went with her friends. I thought it might help."

I offered the grieving mother another small smile. "That was good thinking. Thank you."

"I'm going to start tracking down some leads, but if you get a call from anyone about Lucy, or if you remember anything, don't hesitate to call." I passed her a business card of mine.

Mrs. Bettencourt took the card and nodded, pressing the ever-present handkerchief again to her face. "Thank you," she whispered.

Freyja let me out the front door, but I stopped her with a hand to her arm before she closed it. I handed her one of my cards.

"Call me, anytime," I said, hoping that my eyes conveyed that I wasn't just talking about the case.

The young fae nodded. "Stay safe, Ms. Haley."

Something in her voice told me she wanted to say more, but then the door closed.

I hoped she'd call.

———

I pulled my cell phone out of my pocket as I left the front gates to the Bettencourt property. There were very few numbers I kept on speed dial. Dad, Brigitte, Florentina, and Florentina's grandson. I pressed the fourth number and listened to it ring.

"Mer?" The voice sounded surprised but pleased. It hadn't been *that* long since we'd spoken, had it?

"Hey Sammy," I said. "I need a favor."

"Is this about the Bettencourt kid?"

"Yeah, you heard much about it?" I took a left down the sidewalk, heading toward the streetcar stop.

"Mémé said you were taking the case."

I wasn't surprised Florentina knew I'd accepted the case. She seemed to know everything. I didn't question it.

"What have you heard at the station?"

Samuel hesitated. I heard a glass shatter in the background of the call and a curse. So, he wasn't at the police station today. "Not much, yet, Mer. I'll keep an ear out, though."

"Wait," I said. I could tell he'd been about to hang up. "They took the Bettencourt kid's laptop as evidence. I need the report from it."

A heavy sigh sounded on his side of the phone.

"Pretty please," I intoned.

"I'll see what I can do," I could hear a slur in his voice. "Wait, the kid was taken off Bourbon Street, right?"

"Her mom thought she was at The Rooster. I'm going to go check it out next."

"Wait for me, I'll go with you."

"Sammy—" I sighed. It was just like Samuel LaMontagne to try to keep me from going to places he considered dangerous. Despite me being two years older, he constantly acted like an older brother worried about his little sister.

"No, you shouldn't go on your own," he insisted

I rolled my eyes so far I could've sworn I saw the back of my eye sockets.

"Fine. Meet me at the Agency, and we'll go together. And Sammy?"

"Yeah?"

"Get some strong coffee on the way over. I don't want to smell whatever you've been drinking this afternoon."

I ended the call.

# Chapter Seven

I picked Samuel up at the Agency, grateful that it was only a few streets out of my way to stop for him. The inebriated voice that I had heard on the phone had conjured a far bleaker picture of the owner than the man I picked up. I'd seen visions of three-day stubble and wrinkled band t-shirt. What I hadn't expected was the dark wash jeans, brown leather boots, and light blue dress shirt that answered the Agency's front door before I could open it.

I took a second to hide my surprise.

"Hi." My heightened senses picked up his scent and my eyes narrowed. "Whiskey?"

He flashed me a brilliant smile, extra white against his dark skin. "Coffee?"

"Please."

I stayed put where I was on the front porch, and Samuel hesitated.

"There's nothing good in the kitchen is there?" he asked.

"Nope, you'll have to buy me something."

Samuel stepped out of the building, and let the door shut behind him the small bell chiming as it closed.

"Where we heading?"

"Bourbon Street," I said. "There's coffee on the way."

As we walked, I eyed him over. He'd buzzed his hair short since I'd last seen him. It had been a couple of months, a couple of tragedies ago. I wondered if the haircut had helped him shrug off some of his trauma. I could give a couple of inches of my own locks for that.

"Mer?"

"Yeah?"

"You're staring."

I turned my eyes straight ahead. "I wasn't staring."

A dimple appeared in his right cheek as we walked on. Sometimes I hated that dimple. It was such a familiar look. I'd practically grown up seeing that look. Next to Brigitte, I'd known Samuel the longest in this city. His grandmother renting space at the Agency from my father had only been the beginning. Samuel had become *obsessed* with the work my father had done. The work *I* had done. Him joining NOPD was no surprise when he'd finished high school.

Speaking of—

"Did you have a chance to call the station and get those evidence reports?"

"It's not that simple, Mer," Samuel said. "There's protocols to follow, I can't just show up and demand evidence from an open investigation."

"I'm not sure what's so difficult about it. For me it's two steps. I ask you for the report and you make it happen."

Samuel laughed. It made my heart leap with familiarity. I was drawn to that sound in a way that made me want to grab his hand and hold it while we walked, as though I was sixteen. I could see the weight of the alcohol slipping off him as we walked. He probably didn't need the coffee to sober up, but I did. My guard was slipping around him, and I didn't know why. I needed my senses sharp, especially with the work we had to do.

We stopped at Phyllis' Cafe along the way, hopping off the canal line and walking the rest of the way to Bourbon Street. The Rooster was a newer establishment. Well, new as far as post-portal standards were concerned. It had only been open for a decade or so.

It started as a cafe and bookshop that sometimes hosted live music and slam poetry. Marketing itself toward the younger demographic of Crescent City, it proudly catered to all the residents of New Orleans, not just the human ones. This fact rapidly earned The Rooster a reputation amongst the human parents and not a good one. New ownership in the last few years had leaned into that reputation for profit, and the building was now marketed as an underage club.

I'd heard plenty of the students of Crescent City Academy talking about their exploits here. I was sure if the parents knew all the stories that came out of this building, there'd be far fewer human children among the patrons. Not that I was against the students brushing elbows with the vamps and fae and were-children of the city. It would do many of them good to have empathy for the non-human citizens. Maybe it would make a difference in this place.

It was nearing the evening time when we arrived. On a Friday, I knew they'd want us out of the place as soon as possible to make room for paying customers. It only took a few words to the bouncer before we were seated at a small table near the door and asked to wait for the manager. Samuel took a slow circle, checking out the room. He had been with the NOPD the last two years, I'm sure that kind of surveillance was natural to him. I'd been out of the game for a while now. I hated what that fact made me say next.

"Let me take lead," I said as the bouncer left. "My investigation."

Samuel took his seat and sipped on his coffee. "You're the boss."

I paced the room, looking the place over as Samuel had done.

I would never admit to having come here when I was a teenager, but—man, it had changed over the years. There were still bookshelves, but they had been pushed to the side, now lining the wall across from the bar. A few comfortable-looking couches and chairs sat before them and in the corner creating what looked like a cozy reading nook. The wooden tables and chairs near the entrance seemed to be the only place to sit and eat, as the back of the room was occupied by a massive wooden open floor and a stage. A set of four musicians were on the stage, tuning their instruments and performing a sound check before the night began.

The manager walked over after a few moments and shook our hands. He was young, mid-thirties maybe. He wore black dress pants and leather shoes along with a fitted white button up. Everything about him seemed put together, from the silver watch on his wrist to the full head of brown hair which was swept to the side in a manner that appeared tousled, but I was sure had taken an exorbitant amount of mousse to accomplish.

"Ms. Haley, Mr. LaMontagne, I apologize for keeping you waiting." He gave us a smile that also appeared curated to perfection. Teeth just didn't come that straight on their own. "As you can see, we are preparing for the evening."

I understood the hint he was giving. He wished we'd

come earlier in the day, but he was too polite to say that outright. I counted on that politeness to give us what we wanted.

"We won't take too much of your time Mr.—"

"St. James," he offered.

"Mr. St. James," I attempted a smile to put him at ease. "We just have a few questions for you about Wednesday night. You were here, I assume?"

"I'm here every night."

I held up a picture on my cell phone so he could get a good look. "Did you happen to see Lucy Bettencourt that evening, Mr. St. James?"

The manager barely glanced at the phone. "There were many people here that evening."

Not an answer. Interesting.

Samuel stood and the manager took a step back. Nervous? Not expecting six feet of Cajun to intimidate you?

"Do you have a restroom?" Samuel asked. He gave the manager a sheepish look.

"Second door on the left in the back," St. James said, seeming to recover.

I called his attention back. "Do you have security cameras in the main room here? Pointed out front perhaps?"

The manager gave me a long-suffering look. "Ms. Haley, many of my patrons value their privacy. We make it very clear to our customers that they are responsible for their own selves and belongings while at The Rooster. We take care of the—discretion, of their being here."

I had expected as much. It wasn't only human children who were sneaking away from their parents to spend their evenings here. The vampires, I knew, were also hesitant to allow their children to co-mingle with others in the city.

They sat in their privately secured compounds with their pure bloodlines, and looked down on anything or anyone who might sully their name or reputation or *lineage*. It was no surprise to me that any vamp children would be more comfortable coming here if they knew there would be no record of their having done so.

"We have a camera on the register at the bar and one out back where we receive deliveries," St. James added. "But the footage was all taken by the police department. I'm not sure why I'm going over this for the fourth time. Don't you people talk to each other?"

You people? I bristled at that. I mean sure Samuel was a cop, but I certainly looked nothing like one. Samuel walked back up then, his steps a definitive clomp on the wooden floor, very much like a cop.

I gave the manager a card for Collier Investigations. "If you remember anything, or if someone else here does, please give us a call."

He tucked the card into his shirt pocket. "Is that it?"

"That's it. We'll be back if we have any further questions." I gave him another sweet smile and saw his upper lip twitch. "Thank you for your time."

Samuel and I stepped outside the building, and I shook my head.

"No security cameras, really?"

Samuel shrugged. "I'm sure he has plenty in his office and near whatever he uses as a safe. Why would he care about watching the dumb teens on the dance floor when they're willingly handing cash to him?"

He was probably right. "What'd you get?"

Samuel put a hand to his chest as though offended I would ask. "*I* was in the restroom. This is your investigation after all."

I leveled a hard look on him. "Sammy,"

"Fine, I confess, officer. I talked to the bartender."

"Was he there Wednesday night?"

"Yep." That dimple appeared on his right cheek again. I wanted to flick it.

"And?"

"And he saw Lucy Bettencourt with some friends. They seemed to have a good time. Danced a little and then they left. Separately."

"Separately," I said slowly. "Did she leave with someone else?"

Samuel's eyes twinkled. He was enjoying this too much. "The bartender said a middle-aged man came in as they were getting ready to leave. Lucy went with him."

"Willingly?"

Samuel nodded.

"Someone she knew then." I pushed my hair back from my face and shook it out behind my head, pulling the locks away from my neck in the late summer heat.

"Did you get a description," I asked.

Samuel waved a spiral notebook in front of my face. "I made a sketch."

"Ah, a man of many talents," I looked up and down the street, but no clues jumped out at me. Due diligence, okay? "Let's head back to the Agency. I think dad still has access to the criminal database, we can see if this unknown is in there."

"Lead the way."

My father kept a couch in his office. It was a stained green loveseat with cushions that had permanent impressions on them. No part of that couch looked inviting to sit on, but dad had kept it. Don't ask me why. Maybe it gave him good memories. Maybe sitting in it helped him solve cases. Or maybe he slept on it when whatever case he was working on made him too exhausted to climb the one flight of stairs to his apartment above the office.

My guess was the latter. The second we returned to the Agency, Samuel made his way to that couch, plopped his six-foot frame onto it, flung an arm across his face, and moved no more.

The computer always took ages to boot up. I flipped the switch and headed to the kitchen for some tea. The office door pressed against Samuel's legs when I opened it, but he didn't stir. I returned with some kind of cranberry-based red tea and a gold shawl that Florentina had left over the back of a kitchen chair.

I threw the shawl over Samuel's torso and pulled the spiral notebook out of his breast pocket. A soft snore was his only response to the movement. I paused. Looking down at his sleeping face, I could see signs of wear. Now that he wasn't throwing smiles around like they were free, I could see the lines that dominated the corners of his eyes and mouth. Some were from smiling, sure, but there was more there. A draw in between his eyebrows that had to be caused by some kind of grief or anguish—a past horror he hadn't told me about. Without thinking, I traced my index finger over the lines. His skin was warm beneath my touch, soft. He stirred and I pulled back. Damn fingers had a mind of their own.

The computer had woken up enough to type in the password. I pecked it into the keyboard and waited for the screen to log in. I flipped open the notebook. Samuel hadn't told me not to take it and work on this myself, but still it felt like an intrusion to actually read what he'd recorded. I turned past a couple of pages of nearly illegible writing and a few sketches. I finally found the last page he'd worked on. Our person of interest.

I opened the access to the criminal database on the computer and gave it my father's username and password. We'd worked enough cases together that searching through the database was muscle memory at this point. I input the specifications that Samuel had jotted beside the drawing and searched through the pictures that populated. Why did every white middle-aged male with thinning brown hair look the same in this city?

The tea was good, but this was going to be a long night. I called in an order for food. It was one of those restaurants that cooked a bunch of similar foods and delivered it in paper cartons with forks and chopsticks. Just enough sodium to make Brigitte cringe and give us all a lecture on blood pressure. But she wasn't here to stop me.

Samuel woke up as I brought the food in from the front steps.

"Mm. Chinese," he said, pulling himself vertical with a hand on the back of the couch. I sat cross legged on the two-seater couch, facing him. A half dozen white cartons scattered across our laps and traded between us. Florentina stuck her head in once, liberated a carton of broccoli beef and disappeared again across the hall.

"So, where are we on the unknown guy?" Samuel asked.

I gestured to the pictures I had printed and placed beside the computer. "We'll do a photo lineup with the bartender tomorrow and see if he can point out the guy he saw Wednesday night."

"It's weird there hasn't been a ransom demand." Samuel voiced what had been on my mind. "Do we even know that she was taken? Couldn't she have just, I don't know, been tired of her life and left the city?"

I shrugged. "Her parents seem to think that she wouldn't do that. According to them, they were one big happy family until Wednesday night."

"You don't sound convinced."

"She's a teenage girl."

"Does that necessarily mean she was having problems with her parents?"

I made a 'gimme' motion with my hand until Samuel handed the kung pao chicken over. "You've obviously never been a teenage girl."

He gave a low chuckle. "No, I have to admit, I haven't."

"I suppose it is possible she skipped town. Or..." I trailed off. I didn't want to consider what it might mean if she *was* taken and a ransom call never came. With over a decade of investigative experience, I'd seen enough of what happened when young girls were snatched without a hope of being returned safely. The stories their bodies told, the stories their spirits told—

I shuddered.

"Well, even if she left town of her own volition," I said, "which we don't know, we were hired to investigate. And investigate we shall until we have confirmation one way or another and we can give the Bettencourts some answers."

Samuel raised the paper carton he was holding. "Hear, hear."

I stood before The Rooster with two cups of iced coffee in my hands. The midmorning sun was doing its best to beat a heat record for this season, and my tan tank top wasn't much defense against the burn I was certain would appear on my shoulders later. I had tucked my dark jeans into my working boots and the sweat that was beginning to accumulate at my ankles made me wish desperately that I was spending my morning swimming in one of the nearby lakes rather than working. But there was work to be done and if wishes were fishes—well you know the rest.

I caught sight of Samuel approaching on the sidewalk and checked my watch.

"You're late," I said when he was close enough to hear.

He held up his own plastic cup with a straw. "I stopped for coffee." He looked down at the two drinks in my hands. "You got me coffee."

"No, these are both for me." I took a sip from both straws at once and he rolled his eyes. Those eyes were a golden caramel brown in the sun. I could see a slight sheen of sweat at his temples from the short walk up. It stood out from his dark skin and shimmered in the light.

Samuel threw me a skeptical look. "You're going to get the shakes if you drink all that caffeine."

"I'll be fine," I lied. I hated that he knew me well enough to know that within an hour I'd be a shaking mess if I didn't load up on some kind of food, preferably something salty. Higher metabolism than most of the humans. I processed the caffeine quickly, but that just meant that the detox was heightened.

"Suit yourself." He took an exaggerated sip from his own cup, and I looked away.

"What time did you say he was meeting us here?"

"Eleven forty-five. We've got a few minutes yet."

I'd spent the morning matching demographic information to the photo lineup I had printed yesterday. There hadn't been much on some of the men, records sealed from crimes that the humans didn't care to make public. I doubted NOPD would have given that luxury to the non-human residents of this city that they looked down on and held in derision. Dad's database couldn't give me access to the sealed records. I knew someone who could, I just didn't want to call him. Hopefully the bartender would point out one of the men who had rap sheets long enough to fill a book.

It hadn't made sense to go home for the night since I was using dad's computer for all the information, so I'd stayed on the couch in Dad's office. It wasn't as uncomfortable as it looked, and the combination of incense smell from Tante Flora's shawl and the cologne that Samuel left on the cushions had lulled me to sleep quickly.

Sure, I could have gone upstairs to Dad's apartment for some sleep, but I hadn't been in there since he left. I just couldn't yet.

A side door to the bar swung open on creaking hinges. The man who held it for us was well-muscled, maybe late-twenties, a little over five and a half feet. He wore a faded black t-shirt and jeans.

"Leon," Samuel greeted him, sticking out his hand. "This is Meranda Haley, she's lead on this case."

The bartender gave me a long look from boots to pony-tail. I did my best to look non-threatening. After a moment he shook both our hands and ushered us inside.

The wooden floor echoed our steps in the quiet space. There seemed to be no one else in the building this early in the day, though I was sure it would be bustling soon as the staff prepared for the Saturday night crowd.

"I have a few photos I'd love to have you take a look at, if that's okay, Mr.—"

"Du Gray," the bartender said, stepping behind the bar and giving me a dazzling smile. "And of course I'll look at them."

I reached into the satchel I had slung at my side and pulled out the photographs. As he took them from my outstretched hand, our fingers brushed. It was only for a moment, but Leon's eyes snapped up to mine. I saw a golden glow in the naked bulbs that hung above the bar top. In an instant that glow was gone, but I'd seen enough. A were-creature. The Rooster really was accepting, wasn't it?

He spread the photos out across the bar and stared intently at them one by one. Finally, he tapped a finger on a mugshot from some minor county jail. "This guy. I'm sure of it."

"Would you swear to that in court?" Samuel's question came with the ease of a well-practiced phrase.

I saw Du Gray's hand twitch, a corded muscle in his forearm tightening. The golden flash reappeared in his eyes.

"That won't be necessary," I said quickly, folding the chosen picture in half and tucking it into my back pocket. I pulled the rest of the photos into a loose pile before shoving them back into my bag. "Thank you for your time."

Du Gray nodded once to me, a subtle gesture of gratitude.

I pulled a business card out of the satchel. "If you think of anything else from that night that might be important, or if you see this guy again—"

"I'll call you," the were-thing said, our fingers brushing again as he took my card. His hand lingered near mine for a second too long, and I felt the heat from him. I broke eye contact first.

"Thank you," I said. I stepped back from the bar and placed a hand on Samuel's shoulder. "Let's go."

---

I waited until we were outside of the building and the door had closed behind us, before I shook out my hand. There wasn't a mark on it, but I could feel the place where Du Gray's hand had touched.

"So, what now?" Samuel asked behind me. "Do we head back to the Agency and look this guy up? Make a few calls maybe?"

I pulled out the photo I had folded in half and flipped it over. There wasn't much written on the back. Now I had to make the call I'd been avoiding. Damn it.

"Now, I have a call to make."

Samuel gave me a sideways glance as I pulled out my phone and punched in a number. I paced down Bourbon Street, Samuel in tow as I listened to the ringing on the other end of the line. It was four rings before an answer.

A husky female voice sounding slightly out of breath greeted me. "Hello?"

"Is Oleksandr there?" It wasn't the first time his phone had been answered by some female or another who tagged along with him. I didn't recognize this one's voice, but it had been years since I'd called him up.

"Yes, he's—" her answer was cut off by a sound that was remarkably similar to a phone being snatched out of someone's hand.

"How many times have a told you not to touch the cell phone?" An irritated, but familiar voice sounded. I heard a small slap as though someone had been swatted on the bottom and a tiny yelp. I nearly smiled. That was Oleksandr.

"Hello?"

"Oleksandr," I said, keeping the amusement out of my voice, but just barely.

"Meranda Haley," the voice on the other end breathed out. "I haven't heard from you in years. Now what did I ever do to deserve you not keeping in touch?"

"I know," I said. "I'm sorry, I should have called sooner."

"To what do I owe the pleasure of hearing your voice today?"

"I could use your expertise," I said. Samuel gave me a questioning look and I shook my head to tell him I'd explain later.

"Which expertise do you mean?" Oleksandr purred. "I have several."

I matched his tone, holding the phone close to my mouth as I crooned. "The one involving computers and pesky passwords and unbreachable firewalls."

"Oh," came the flat reply. "That one."

"Judging by the voice that first answered your phone, whose owner I am certain is drop dead gorgeous, I don't think your other specialties are going to waste."

A heavy sigh sounded on the other end of the line. "Where do you want to meet?"

"There's a bar off Bourbon Street called Baxter's. Do you know it?"

"I've heard of it. Today?"

"Pretty please."

"I'll have to rearrange some things."

"I'll buy you all the Bloody Mary's you could possibly want."

Samuel made a choking noise behind me, but I ignored him.

"Oh darling," Oleksandr's voice was smooth as satin. "You don't have the means to pay that bill."

"You'll come anyway?" I asked. "I promise to call more often."

"You're a cruel woman," Oleksandr said. "And a tease. But I'll be there."

"See you soon," I said and hung up the phone.

I turned to face Samuel, steeling myself for the glower I was sure he would give me.

"You can't promise a resource 'all the Bloody Mary's he could want'," Samuel said flatly.

"Is there a law against it, Officer?"

"No," Samuel said, looking up the street. "It just makes you look desperate."

I smiled.

"Now where are we heading?"

"Now," I said, shoving my phone back in my pocket. "You're buying me lunch."

"What? How did that become my job?"

"You wanted to tag along on the investigation," I said, shrugging my shoulders as though what I was saying was a truth universally acknowledged. "Rookie buys the food."

Samuel let out a grumbling noise.

"Come on, Baxter's is only a couple blocks up the street."

"What's a Baxter?"

"You'll see."

# Chapter Eight

"So that's a Baxter."

I looked over at the bulldog snoring on the bar top. "That's a Baxter."

Samuel pushed an index finger along the bar before lifting it to inspect the tip. "It doesn't seem all that sanitary."

"Have a beer," I said. "It'll make you feel better about it."

Samuel made a grumbling noise again. This was becoming a bad habit of his. I wondered if I should talk to Florentina about it. Maybe he was coming down with something.

"Mer," Charlie greeted me with a smile that nearly split his face in two. "Can I get you the usual?"

"Sure, Charlie, and whatever lunch special you have going."

"Can I get anything for your fella?"

Samuel made a choking noise. "Uh, no, I'm not—, I'll have whatever she's getting."

I put a hand on Charlie's arm. "Bring him a beer."

Charlie gave me a conspiratory wink. "You got it."

I pulled out the photo that Leon had pointed to and flipped it over. Samuel twisted in his barstool. It emitted a small, tortured squeak with each move to the left.

"Would you cut it out?"

"No, this thing needs some oil or something."

"Maybe it needs a beer too," I murmured, reading the scanty demographics I had written on the back of the mug shot.

Peter Grassi. Fifty-six years old. That's it. That's all I had, aside from the photo.

I stroked Baxter's ears as we waited and ignored Samuel who was crouched down on the floor now, peering up at the underside of the stool and turning it back and forth. The bar was almost empty at noon on a Saturday which surprised me. I didn't visit Baxter's all too often in the middle of the day, but I'd always assumed the place was crowded no matter what the time was. That was okay, though. Oleksandr would prefer the privacy.

I turned to Samuel who had finally given up on finding the source of the squeak and sat on the stool beside me. "Did you get a chance to call about the police reports? Where are they in the investigation?"

"I told you, Mer. It's not that simple."

I opened my mouth to protest, but Charlie walked up.

"A beer for the mister," Charlie said, passing a pint of amber colored liquid to Samuel. "And your usual. Be right back with the food."

I murmured my thanks as the glass of clear liquid came to a rest before me. A few bubbles dislodged from their hold on the inside of the cup and floated to the surface, popping with a confetti-like spray.

"Vodka soda?" Samuel asked, eying my drink.

"Something like that," I said, noting that he hadn't fully

answered the question about NOPD's evidence, and now he was trying to change the subject.

"I'd really like those police reports," I said. "I let you tag along on this investigation because I thought you'd be an asset."

That wasn't fair of me. He *had* gotten the bartender to cooperate, but I couldn't understand why he wouldn't make one phone call to his friends and get us what we needed.

"Drop it, Mer," Samuel's tone was a warning. "I'll get you the reports when I work next."

"When's that?" I pressed.

Samuel's eyes shone with irritation. "Monday, okay? I'll get them for you Monday."

We glared at each other for a moment and Charlie set two plates of burgers and fries down before us without interrupting the staring contest. He really was an excellent barkeep.

I broke eye contact, finally. "Let's eat. I'm starving."

"Warned you not to drink both of those coffees," Samuel said, and we pretended the tension was gone between us.

Samuel and I both looked up at the mirror behind the bar as we heard the door to Baxter's swing open. In the reflection, it looked as though the wind had pushed it as no one strode through the opening, but I knew that wasn't true. I smiled down at my glass as Samuel twisted in his seat to double check the front door. I could feel him tense beside me as the newcomer approached our barstools bypassing the rest of the empty bar.

"Meranda Haley," The cool voice sounded behind me. It was the kind of voice you'd expect to read poetry in a darkened room where people paid ridiculous prices for only a half-decent latte. The kind of voice that when whispered in the dark, made people's hearts leap in their chests in an unfamiliar mixture of fear and arousal.

"Oleksandr Kieran," I said and swiveled the barstool around to face him. The stool let out a squeak of protest and I mentally cursed it for ruining a perfectly melodramatic meeting.

"Kieran?" Samuel asked beside me. I could hear the surprise in his voice, the mental calculations that were going on in his head as he took in the image before us.

Oleksandr Kieran was a contrast of dark and light. Like a Rembrandt, he'd tell you. Chiaroscuro. He was dramatic that way.

Tailored black dress slacks clothed his lower half leading to matte black dress shoes. A black dress shirt tucked into his waistband, held in place by a dark leather belt. The skin of his face was so pale, you almost wouldn't believe him to be healthy, but that was the price you had to pay when the sun scorched your skin. Cheekbones that could have been chiseled from marble cast shadows on his jawline and above them dark eyes regarded me framed by longer lashes than seemed fair for one person to possess.

I could see the handle of the dark umbrella he'd tucked under his left arm that had protected him from the high noon glare. He held a black leather briefcase on the same side as the umbrella. An expensive looking silver watch peeked out from his shirtsleeve.

It was a far cry from the penniless, near starving shell of a creature who had turned up on my father's doorstep over a decade ago.

"I didn't think you were back in the game," Oleksandr said, his eyes glinting with unspoken curiosity.

"I'm not," I said. "Just this one case."

The vampire raised an eyebrow but didn't push the point.

"Kieran," Samuel repeated, more slowly this time. It wasn't common to see a vampire operating outside of the safety of their compounds, but it wasn't entirely unheard of. If Samuel was going to keep up in this world, he'd have to get quicker with his vampire trivia.

Oleksandr fixed him with dark eyes. "Something to say, officer?" His lips drew back as he spoke, giving a glimpse of sharpened canines.

Samuel bristled beside me. "How's your grand-mère?"

Perhaps not so ignorant of vampire lineage as I had initially thought. Victoria Kieran was the head of one of the most powerful vampire clans in the city. She ruled her family with the same iron grip she held over her myriad of businesses. Her brutality and swift justice were legend on this side of the city. Most who crossed her were never heard from again. Oleksandr's exile was a rare exception. I was sure the reminder of his grandmother did not endear Samuel to him.

The tension grew between the two of them. Oleksandr's lips were still drawn back, and Samuel leaned forward, seeming ready to try his hand at matching the superhuman strength of his opponent if it came to that. I leaned back against the bar behind me. It wasn't my job to keep them in line. They were grown ass adults.

Charlie appeared behind my shoulder and set a Bloody Mary on the counter beside me. The scent of tomato and vodka filled the air. Oleksandr sniffed once, pulling air into lungs that had no need of oxygen. He paused his staring contest long enough to cast a longing glance at the glass of red liquid beside me. I saw his lips softening into a smile rather than a snarl.

"Truce?" I asked, holding the glass out to him.

"Truce," Oleksandr agreed. He looked at the empty barstool beside me and the spot where Baxter snored on the bar top above it. "But I will not be sitting beside the dog."

"Fair enough," I said.

Samuel switched seats without protest and seemed to make a point of scratching the bulldog's head as he slept, telling him what a good boy he was. Oleksandr took the vacated stool on my right.

"I was surprised to get your call," he said, pointedly ignoring Samuel.

"I was surprised to have called you," I said.

"Didn't expect you to return to the streets after what happened."

I got control of the shudder before it had a chance to wrack my body and took a deep breath through my nose, grounding myself to this place, the food before me. *What happened* still woke me up some nights and left me in a cold sweat. It was a dick move of Oleksandr to bring it up even if he'd been there. I knew he was testing me, gauging how much it still impacted me.

I wouldn't let him see it.

Oleksandr could be trusted for his competency, but I knew better than to give him a glimpse into myself. His business was information, and I didn't know who his other clients may be. The less truth he knew about me, the better.

"I called you for your expertise," I said.

"Right to business." His dark eyes gleamed in the light that reflected off the mirror above the bar, the one that couldn't show his image. He set his briefcase on the bar top and unfastened the clasps with a click. I passed the photo to him once he'd gotten the laptop out of the case.

Oleksandr Kieran was one of the few hackers in this city

who could route past the NOPD firewalls. If anyone could get me information on Peter Grassi, it would be him. Normally, the charges would be too high for me to use his services. I didn't know if our previous arrangement still applied, but even if it didn't, the Bettencourts were footing the bill. If they got Lucy back, I was sure they'd be more than happy to pay his fee.

"Peter Grassi," Oleksandr murmured, reading the back of the photo.

"You know him?"

"Never heard of him," the vampire said, turning his attention to the computer before him. He pulled out a pair of dark framed glasses from the case and slipped them on. They made him look older. Sophisticated, even. As though he'd stand in an art gallery and explain paintings to younger females as part of a mating ritual. I almost laughed at the visual. I didn't hate the look though. Most vampires were handsome in their own right, but the familiarity of the one beside me, the years we'd spent working together— the glasses added to the handsome, I concluded. Even if they were just for blocking blue light.

I let him clack away on the keyboard for a few minutes and focused on my burger. Charlie was an artist. That or I was just hungry. Either way, I would sing the praises of this bar until the day I died. Samuel watched Oleksandr as he worked. I could tell he was sizing the vampire up, trying to find weaknesses in the hard as ice exterior. It's diamonds, I almost whispered. Oleksandr Kieran had a soft spot for shiny jewels and freshly procured pearls. Objects that I'd had access to once upon a time, but no more.

Oleksandr turned the screen to face me and picked up his drink, sipping quietly from the straw. I pulled the laptop closer. The mugshot of Peter Grassi occupied the left side of the screen. A banner across the top of the page showed that we were in the New Orleans Police Department's database.

"Now wait a minute," Samuel protested behind me.

"Are you going to march down to the station and get me the information I need?" I asked, not taking my eyes off the screen.

"Well, no, but—"

"Hush, then," I said, scrolling down to the Known Addresses section.

Samuel fell silent, but I could hear him breathing harder behind me. I couldn't care about that, though. There was a kid missing.

I jotted down the current address that was listed for Grassi and scrolled down to known charges. He'd had a few citations, one arrest for domestic violence for which the charges had been dropped. A few altercations with previous employers. It wasn't enough to land him in jail for long, but he'd definitely spent a few nights behind bars for violence. The man had a temper. And he'd been the last one seen with Lucy Bettencourt.

I passed the laptop back to Oleksandr with a murmured thanks.

"Anything else?" Oleksandr asked, his eyes glinting again.

"That's it," I said. "Thanks for meeting us, I know it's an inconvenience." I gestured to the bright sunlight that streamed through the windows at the front of the bar.

Oleksandr smiled, his canines showing again. "Anything for you, Meranda."

Most were unnerved by the image of those teeth. It reached directly to a fear that primeval humans had structured into their DNA; from a time when fire was the only protection this species had against the children of the night. I matched his smile, knowing that this too was a test of his.

He put the laptop back in the case and latched it. I watched as he knocked back the rest of his drink and stood with near silent ease.

"I'm sure I will see you again soon," he said.

"I told you," I said. "It's just the one case."

Oleksandr inclined his head once to me and then gave Samuel a glower before striding out of the bar, opening his umbrella as he exited.

"I don't like him," Samuel said.

"Really?" I asked. "You hid it so well."

Samuel shrugged and took a long draught of his beer.

I looked down at the information I'd written from Peter Grassi's file.

It wasn't completely surprising that he'd been on Bourbon Street Wednesday night. Plenty of people drove into the city for the evening chasing the bar scene. What I'd like to know was how he knew the Bettencourts, Lucy specifically. Her parents didn't paint her as the type of kid who'd get into the car with a complete stranger, and the bartender had said it seemed as though they knew each other. I may have to pay another visit to Mr. and Mrs. Bettencourt. Maybe it was a family friend who wasn't at all involved with Lucy's disappearance. Maybe he was the last one to see her and he'd be more than happy to answer questions about it.

I had to check with the Bettencourts first, then we could check out Peter Grassi's current address. I really wanted to talk to this Peter guy. Even if he'd dropped Lucy off somewhere and hadn't been a part of her going missing, he could point me to another place she'd been that night.

I shoved the last few french fries into my mouth. "Let's head back to the Agency," I said. "We've got calls to make."

The second we arrived at the Agency Florentina stole Samuel away to help with some handyman work she needed done in her parlor. I made my way into Dad's office and sat behind the desk.

I pulled up the number I had for the Bettencourts and leaned back in the wheeled chair.

The phone was answered on the second ring.

"Bettencourt residence,"

I recognized the voice. "Freyja, it's Meranda Haley. May I speak to Mr. or Mrs. Bettencourt, please?"

"Just a moment." The reply was curt, professional.

Another voice spoke into the phone. "Hello,"

"Mrs. Bettencourt," I said. "Meranda Haley—"

Mrs. Bettencourt cut me off before I could say anything else. "Did you find her? Do you have Lucy?"

"No ma'am," I said. I couldn't imagine the hurt my words were causing, but I heard the strangled sniff that sounded from her end of the phone. "We're still looking. A name came up in our investigation, a Mr. Peter Grassi..." I trailed off, hoping Mrs. Bettencourt would understand my question.

"Peter Grassi," Louisa Bettencourt said the name slowly as though thinking through it as she spoke. "Yes, I believe that's—Robert! What's Uncle Petey's last name?"

I heard a muffled reply to her question and then she was back on the phone. "Yes, we've known Peter for years. You don't believe he's somehow involved in this, do you?" I could hear her voice rising into a near hysteria. "You don't think he took her!"

"His name just came up, Mrs. Bettencourt," I assured her. "I don't know if he's involved or not, yet. Would you happen to have a current address or a phone number for him?"

"Yes, I believe I do." I heard some rustling on the other line as though she was flipping through a booklet of some kind. She came back on the line and rattled off the information for me. I jotted it down.

"When was the last time you or Mr. Bettencourt saw Mr. Grassi?"

"Oh, it's been years. We had him over for Christmas, what was it, two years ago?" A muffled confirmation. "Yes. Two years ago. Haven't seen him since. He travels a bit, I believe."

"Thank you, Mrs. Bettencourt."

"You'll call me if you find anything?"

"Yes ma'am."

We hung up and I looked over the address she had given me. It didn't match the one that had been in the database. Now I had two places to visit. I figured I could call the phone number first, but I was worried that if he was involved, our talking would just tip him off to get the hell out of Dodge and I couldn't risk that. It was much easier to keep ahold of a suspect if you had them in person rather than on the phone.

I walked across the hallway and into the parlor. My aunt was sitting at her small table. The crimson tablecloth draped to the floor and covered her bottom half. A purple cloth covered over a dome shape in the center of the table which I knew was the crystal ball she used with some clients. Florentina didn't look up as I entered. The tall candles cast imposing shadows along her face. She was flipping cards on the table, reading tarot.

"I sent him out," my aunt said by way of greeting.

"Okay." I slid into the chair across from her and tried not to look at the cards she was reading. There was much I found fascinating about my aunt, many powers I found useful and would even seek out, but fortunes? Prophecies? Not a chance.

"Your defenses are low."

I knew what she meant. Before I left my father's work, Florentina had been teaching me ways to shield myself from the spirits around me. How to only attract and interact with the ones I wanted, and repel the others. The static, she'd called it.

"I haven't needed them."

"Until you do," she said pointedly.

I looked away. Her parlor really was magnificent. The walls were covered in thick richly colored curtains that made it difficult to determine the exact size and shape of the room. In fact, most of the decorations in here were made to throw off someone's perception. A mirror hung on the wall behind Tante Flora, covered with a gray gauzy scarf, so the reflections shone fuzzy, and the dancing candlelight seemed infinite.

"How is the case?" Florentina asked, her eyes still trained on the cards before her.

"It's going as all other cases do, we ask questions, we get answers. Sometimes we even get the truth."

A half smile quirked the side of Florentina's face. "You make jokes."

"I make jokes."

Florentina collected the cards into a neat stack and slid

them into a velvet bag. "You can always ask for help if the jokes don't work."

"You hate the messiness of our cases," I pointed out.

"I wasn't talking about me, girl."

I stopped short. "I'm not asking Dad for help."

Florentina adjusted a golden ring on her left hand, a massive sapphire graced its center. "It's one long distance call."

"I'm not talking to him yet."

"Suit yourself," my aunt rose. "But when you're looking for help, and you don't know where to turn, he'll be there."

I followed Tante Flora into the kitchen, hating the way her words hung like a prophecy in the air.

Florentina made some tea and we sat at the kitchen table.

"Where did you say Samuel went?"

"He's helping me hang something," Florentina waved a hand, white bangles clinking as she did so. "We didn't have the right hanging things."

"Screws?"

"Whatever it is you use these days."

I nearly laughed. Sometimes Florentina spoke as though she had been around for centuries. With how little I truly knew about her past, I supposed it was possible, but to have a grandson my age—I doubted it. It was far more likely her head was filled with too many other things. More important things having to do with magic and foretelling. She had no space for such inconsequential information as the proper name for hanging things.

I thanked her as she placed the teacup before me.

"I could teach you again, you know?" My aunt said, taking her seat across from me.

"I know." Memories of why I gave up my spiritual

defense lessons flitted through my mind, and I leaned into the spicy aroma of the tea, dispelling the thoughts as I overloaded another sense.

"It wouldn't have to be like last time. You are older now. You've lived longer with your abilities. You could have more control."

"I'm fine, Tante," I said, giving her a smile I didn't feel. "I should be spending all my time on this case. There's still a girl missing."

"No ransom yet?" Florentina asked and took a sip of her tea.

I shook my head.

The air whistled through her teeth as Florentina drew in a sharp breath and shook her head. She knew as well as I that the lack of ransom demand didn't bode well for Miss Lucy Bettencourt.

"I will light a candle for her safe return."

I nodded. "You do that, and I'll go out and get her."

# Chapter Nine

I met Samuel outside the Agency the following morning. I didn't know his current address, but Sammy insisted the small building was the midway point between our places. I double checked the set of keys I held and led him around back. There was a tiny parking lot behind the Agency, one four-door gray sedan the only car there. I pushed a button on my keys and the lights blinked on and off.

"He left you the car too?"

"He must have thought I'd need it for the Agency."

"So, it's a company car." Samuel's voice was a tease, as though I wore a suit and went to an office every day to sit behind a desk and push papers.

"I'm very important you know." I yanked the driver's door open. "Get in. You're navigating."

I handed Samuel the paper on which I'd written the two addresses. Starting with the address from the NOPD database, we left the parking lot, and I turned the car west. It always felt strange to drive in this city. Ever since I was a small child, I'd walked these streets, took public transport; I hardly ever drove. The lanes always seemed too narrow when you were in a car as though they were made for a time before personal vehicles were a thing. I had the sudden image of horses and buggies driving on these streets. They'd probably fit fine.

"Turn left up here," Samuel said. "Get on the I-10."

I took the turn and suddenly horses and buggies didn't make sense anymore as the highway stretched before me.

Plenty of the interstates across the country were destroyed by the portals. The spaces in between major cities had become too dangerous to travel, as creatures who had only been spoken of in lore took over the less populated areas. Even now, if you got far enough west, civilization disappeared in favor of a lawless country where might made right, and claws and fangs determined victors. Only the Rangers were brave enough, or dumb enough, to traverse that harsh terrain now. Rarely, they brought other travelers safely through.

The Louisiana town that held the first address was near enough to the city that the highway was intact. Samuel directed me to pull off the interstate and we took a left at the first intersection. In no time, we crossed bridges that spanned bayous and lakes. Someone long ago had the bright idea to plant houses along the edges of the water, as though the wetland wasn't a vicious and claiming thing. Wooden docks extended into the water from the rundown shacks. Most of the structures looked unoccupied now, but one never knew. It wouldn't surprise me if they were owned by non-humans these days—creatures that had been forced from the city proper by those who felt they were better than those around them, and a law enforcement that let them fall through the cracks.

We pulled off the paved road and onto a dirt path.

Several ramshackle structures dotted either side of the dirt, spaced well enough apart that they wouldn't disturb their neighbors. The hovels had been slapped together with whatever spare wood and metal siding was available at the time. Many sagged and tilted as though the swamp was trying to swallow them up but was taking its sweet time doing so. We pulled to a stop at the second to last house.

"This is it?"

Samuel gave me a shrug. "Near as I can tell. Not too many house numbers out here."

The second we exited the car, my senses were assaulted by the bayou. Insects buzzed all around us. The sound of a bullfrog doing its best impression of a lounge singer accosted my ears. I closed my eyes and took a moment to get my senses under control as the smells wafted around me, green and wet and warm. I could feel *them* too, the spirits of the swamp. They lingered under the water—waiting, watching, wanting.

"You good?" Samuel stood beside me then. He touched a hand to my elbow.

I breathed in his scent, his cologne a familiar blend of sandalwood and teak. It centered me.

"I'm good," I said, opening my eyes. "Let's go."

The door to the shack was still attached to the wooden frame by one hinge and a good amount of optimism. I opted to knock on the doorframe.

We waited a long moment, but no one answered.

"Hello?" Samuel called.

Still no answer. We walked around to the back of the sagging building. The dock wasn't in much better shape. Half of it dipped into the water and sludge of the bayou, looking like nothing so much as it was being consumed by the bog. I wouldn't trust my own weight on it, and I was pretty sure it hadn't seen a boat in years.

"Who're ye? What're ye doing here?"

I turned at the harsh voice. The owner stood a good ten feet away and didn't look as though she had any intention of coming closer. She was petite, dirt smudged across her small face and patched clothes. Her boots looked as though they had seen better days, and her hair hung in greasy locks around her pointed ears. A lesser fae, then, like Freyja. She probably had a tie to the bayou magic.

"We're looking for Peter Grassi," I said, not stepping closer so as not to scare her. "We were told he lived here."

"N'one's lived 'ere for years." The woman crossed her arms over her chest. "We din't like strangers."

"Do you know who owns this place?" Samuel asked.

"Nae," the fae said. She cast an eye toward the water. "Git 'fore a rusalka gets ye."

I raised an eyebrow. There was no rusalki nearby. I would have sensed them as surely as I could feel the spirits below the surface of the swamp.

"Is there someone else we could talk to?" Samuel asked. He took a step forward and the fae vanished. Fae didn't vanish, of course, but they sure moved quickly when they wanted to.

"I don't think there's anyone else," I said and put a hand on Samuel's arm. We looked up the row of houses, the small faces that peered out of their windows. Not a one of them friendly. "Let's check out the next address on the list."

We drove back up the dirt path after a complicated seven-point turn at the end of the row. Eyes watched us from the windows of each occupied shack until we were out of sight.

We drove for a while in silence, neither of us able to shake the feeling that going to that address was a complete waste of time. Samuel gave directions again as we neared New Orleans proper. We turned south.

"We could have looked inside the cabin," Samuel said in between directions. "Just taken a look around. Even if no one was home."

I thought back to the sagging porch and broken windows. "If I thought anyone had been there for years, we would have. Did you see those neighbors? I don't think they would have looked very kindly on two city slickers poking around their street. And aren't there rules against breaking and entering, Mr. Cop?"

Samuel shrugged and turned to look out the window. He didn't speak to me again until it was time to turn off the highway, and he directed me toward a neighborhood of cement and multi-floored apartment buildings.

"We're here?" I asked as we pulled to a stop on the curbside.

"This is the address." Samuel eyed my parallel parking skills with a critical eye. There was nothing to object to. Dad taught me to do that well, at least.

We both looked up at the set of apartments as we left the car. The building was a cookie cutter version of three more on the street. Veritably boring compared to the address from which we'd come. It stood three stories high, cracked white paint coating the outside. Every other set of windows on the second and third floors had a balcony leading out to the glorious view of the unkempt asphalt below.

"Don't suppose they have an elevator in this place," Samuel mused by my side.

"It's not the Ritz," I said. "You're afraid of a few stairs, copper?"

"No." The defensive tone was back. "I just like to know what my options are."

I looked back at the dilapidated front of the building. "Fair."

The address was on the second floor. A set of rickety stairs with a suspicious looking banister led us up. The apartment was halfway down the hall. Doors we passed all looked the same save for the black numbers painted on the front. Normal apartment sounds muffled by the wooden doors made their way into the hall. A dog barking, a baby crying, a couple fighting. It brought back memories of when Dad and I had first arrived in the Crescent City, and all we could afford was a rundown apartment. Dad had bought deadbolts and chains that we didn't have permission to affix to the walls and said, to hell with the landlord, I'm keeping my kid safe.

I wondered how many parents, down on their luck but viciously protecting their children had done the same behind these walls. Some looked down on people who lived in certain buildings just due to the look of the building itself, but I knew better than anyone that all kinds lived behind these walls. Loving parents, paroled rapists, domestic abusers, and abuse survivors. Judging someone for where they came from was ridiculous to me, but looking over at Samuel's grimace as we passed a door where a couple was fighting, I knew he wouldn't understand. His time at the police academy and working the streets made him view the world differently from me. I wasn't sure I liked that.

Door 223 was before us at last and Samuel knocked.

"Coming," a cheerful voice sounded from inside. Not the kind of voice I expected from someone who had spent a turn at the county jail, but who was I to judge.

The door swung open, and a man of average height stared out into the hall. "May I help you?"

He wore tan slacks with a dark green polo shirt tucked in. His brown hair was swept to the side and affixed there with a gel or hairspray. His face was clean shaven and dark-rimmed square glasses sat on the bridge of his nose. He looked like nothing so much as a professor who golfed on the weekends. Looking at him, you'd never think he had charges on his record.

"Peter Grassi?" I asked.

"Yes,"

"I'm Meranda Haley, this is Samuel. We're representatives from Collier Investigations. We'd like to ask you a few questions."

"Ah, I expected there was more than one of you, come on in."

More than one of us?

His voice remained cheerful, as though we were neighbors who had come for a cup of sugar, and he stepped aside so we could enter.

"After you," I gestured for Mr. Grassi to lead the way. I'd been out of the game for a few years, but even I knew not to give my back to a suspect.

Peter Grassi didn't look offended in the slightest. He led us into the square living space. Just as Grassi's attire, the living area was impeccably clean and tidy. A clear vase holding sunflowers sat on a low table in the center of the room. A three-seater couch faced the television. Two armchairs sat to the left of it, their backs to the window overlooking the street, and in the armchairs—

"Ms. Haley." The greeting was friendly enough, but I scowled.

"Mr. Georgiano," I said. "Jr." The second man nodded to me.

I'd dealt with the Georgianos for years. A father-son team, their private investigative agency had been a thorn in my father's side almost since he first opened Collier Investigations. They had a reputation for getting results regardless of whether or not their methods would stand up in court. A favorite resource of many of the criminal organizations in New Orleans who didn't *need* evidence to stand up, just names to off.

I could hardly blame the Bettencourts for hiring more than one agency. If it was my kid missing, I'd hedge my bets too, but this did complicate our work beyond what was tolerable. The chances that we would be here at the same time, that evidence wouldn't be messed up by the time we got to it if the Georgianos ever got ahead of us...

"Please, sit, sit." Grassi was pulling a chair from beside the table in the kitchenette. "This will be so much easier to go over just once."

Samuel dropped onto the couch. I sat stiffly beside him, trying to keep his considerably heavier weight from creating a hole in the cushions and sucking me down to his side.

"What is it you want to go over, Mr. Grassi?" I asked. I had no idea what he may have told the Georgianos before we arrived, but I certainly wasn't going to stay ignorant.

Peter Grassi waved a hand through the air as though dispelling smoke from about him. "Well, as soon as I'd seen that Lucy was missing, I knew it was only a matter of time before someone came looking for me."

"So, you admit to seeing Lucy Bettencourt on Wednesday evening?" The older Georgiano asked. Franklin Georgiano's voice was older than I remembered, weathered. The lines on his face were much deeper than I had last seen him. I was sure under the brown driver cap he wore, his graying hair would be thinner too.

"Of course," Peter Grassi laughed. "I could hardly deny it."

"Well, Mr. Grassi," I said. "It seems you're the last person who has seen her. Why don't you walk us through what you did after you picked her up."

I caught Georgiano Jr. sneering at me from the corner of my eye, but I ignored him.

"There isn't much to tell," Grassi began. "I picked her up from one of those strange underage establishments in the city and dropped her off back home. It didn't feel right letting her walk home that late."

"How did you know she'd be there?" I asked quickly, beating the Georgianos to the next question.

"Her father called me," Grassi said. "Didn't he tell you that?"

No, he had not. Interesting.

"We corroborate everything we hear, Mr. Grassi," I said.

Georgiano Sr. appeared to have had enough of me being in charge. His voice boomed louder than necessary in the small apartment. "Where did you drop the girl off?"

The girl has a name, I thought, but listened closely for the reply.

"I dropped her off on the street to her house. She didn't want me to alert her mom that she had been out, so I didn't ring the bell to bring my car up the driveway," Peter Grassi paused. His throat worked past a lump, his dark eyes glassing with moisture. "I should never have left her alone."

"No, you shouldn't have," the younger Georgiano said shortly. "That still leaves you as the last to see her that night." His tone was a threat. Odd. Bad form. He would spook Grassi if he kept that up. Pleasant witnesses were more reliable. When people were panicked that they were a serious suspect, they were more likely to make up a story that painted themselves in a kinder light.

"I'm sure you didn't mean for anything to happen to her," I said, hoping my voice was placating. "How did Mr. Bettencourt know to call you? Why didn't he call someone who lived in the city?"

Peter Grassi snorted. "Richard and I go way back. I knew him long before he married Louisa; long before he had any kind of reason to save face."

I raised an eyebrow at him, prompting more.

"He called me precisely because I wasn't in the city. I'm not associated with his life there. He could trust that I wouldn't ruin his *precious* reputation."

Not resentful about our good friend moving on to bigger and better things. Nope, not in the slightest.

"So let me make sure I have this straight," Samuel said. "You received a call from Richard Bettencourt that his daughter had snuck out, and without a question you dropped everything to drive twenty miles into the city. You pick up the girl and drop her off on her street and you just— go home?"

Peter Grassi pushed his glasses up his forehead and rubbed at his eyes. "Basically, yes."

"And you did this out of the kindness of your heart? A favor to an old friend?"

"Yes."

Georgiano Jr. spoke up again. "I'm sure the ten thousand dollars that Mr. Bettencourt deposited in your account had nothing to do with it."

I schooled my face into neutrality. They didn't have to know that we hadn't learned about that. Dammit. If we'd had access to police resources as we were *supposed* to, we could have had that information before driving over here.

"I do odd jobs for Richard all the time. It is not out of the ordinary for him to pay me for them," Peter Grassi said, unfazed by the question. "If you review the bank statements that you obviously have access to, you'd see that I've collected from him a couple times a year for the last five years or so."

Mrs. Bettencourt had assured me that they hadn't seen 'Uncle Petey' in years. Did she not know that her husband used him so frequently or was she just lying to protect him? And protect him from what?

"When was the last time you saw the Bettencourts?" I asked.

"I took Richard on a fishing trip over the summer," he said after a moment's thought. "He likes to unwind away from the city."

"You went to your cabin near Manchac?" I asked and received immense satisfaction from the surprise I caught on the younger Georgiano's face before he got his expression under control. They hadn't known about it, then. Turnabout and fair play and all that.

Grassi, too, looked surprised we knew about the cabin. "We fish up there together all the time. I'm sure if you asked Mr. Bettencourt about it, he would tell you the same."

He didn't know that we'd visited the cabin. He didn't know that we'd seen how dilapidated it was, how apparent that no one had visited it for years. Which raised the question: if not fishing, what were he and Mr. Bettencourt doing together over the summer?

"Now, if you don't have any other questions," Mr. Grassi rose. "I need to be getting ready for work."

He was cutting us short. He didn't like us asking about the cabin.

"Of course, Mr. Grassi," I said. "Thank you for your time."

The Georgianos didn't look happy about being pushed out, but they didn't seem to have any other questions either. At least, no more that they felt comfortable asking with us present also. It wouldn't surprise me if they intended to approach Mr. Grassi again when we weren't there. In their shoes, I'd do the same.

The four of us filed out into the hall together. I didn't like the idea of the Georgianos walking behind me, but Samuel put his hand on my shoulder, assuring me that he was there. The door closed behind us and suddenly the older Georgiano was in my face.

"I knew your father had fallen on hard times, but he must really be desperate to have sent you to handle his cases."

His hot breath hit me like a gust from a furnace, but I stood my ground.

"Franklin, you know I've worked these sorts of cases since I could walk." I tried to sound as bored as possible. "Pulling your son out of business school to join you in your ventures, though," I tsked at him. "What disarray must your house be in."

"Hey," Georgiano Jr. began, but his father held up a hand, stopping him short.

"My son is a perfectly fine investigator, and I don't like what you're insinuating Ms. Haley."

An image of baseball sized stones and glass houses flitted through my brain. "Yes, Franklin, I'm sure Darryl is *adequate*." I knew that would piss him off, and I stepped back as Georgiano Jr. made a grab for my shirt front. In a blink, Samuel had the younger man against the wall, a forearm across his chest.

"You do not touch her," my knight in well-fitted button up hissed.

"Call off your guard dog," Franklin said.

"Keep your son on a leash, Franklin," I said sweetly. "And I won't have to."

"Darryl, you walk in front of me." Mr. Georgiano said.

Samuel let the younger Georgiano off the wall, and he slunk before us. If he had a tail, it would be between his legs.

"Don't think I don't know the real reason you brought your kid home," I said softly. "I'm sure there are plenty at the university who want that story."

Georgiano Sr. held up his hands in a placating gesture and gave me a generous smile. The man knew when to quit, I'd give him that.

Still, I was grateful for Samuel's presence at my side.

"I'm afraid this case may be too small for both of our agencies to be working on it," Mr. Georgiano said as we descended the stairs.

"I was about to say the same thing," I said, preparing to fight for our rights to it. We needed the payout. I wasn't going to just give it up.

Mr. Georgiano stopped on the ground floor, waved his son on, and turned to face me. "It's yours."

"That easy?" I asked, not allowing myself to lower my guard yet.

"Yes, that easy," Mr. Georgiano's smile was magnanimous and fake. So, so fake. "I'm sure you'll agree that my son needs an—" he searched for the right word, "—uncomplicated case to welcome him back to the game."

I gave him an artificial smile of my own. "Of course. It is only proper to start your progeny off on the right foot."

"Indeed." Georgiano began walking again. "I wish you luck with the case, Ms. Haley. Tell your father I said hello when you see him next."

I tried not to let the barb find its mark. I didn't know how much he knew about my father's status. We pushed out the front doors of the apartment building and stepped onto the scorching sidewalk. "Thank you, Mr. Georgiano. Good luck with your work as well."

Georgiano gave a noncommittal noise and took his leave of us, sliding into an expensive looking black car. Its windows were tinted against scrutiny, but I could see the silhouette of Darryl Georgiano in the driver's seat. I gave him a friendly wave and he responded with a less than friendly gesture back.

"Let's go," I said.

We pulled the car away from the curb and back to the main streets before I spoke again. "We should have known about the money transfer," I said softly.

Samuel's jaw was working, but he didn't look at me.

"If we'd had access to the police department resources, we would have been better prepared," I said.

"Maybe you should have asked your bloodsucker friend."

He held up a hand as though realizing that the harsh tone was unwarranted. "It's not that simple, Mer. You'd need warrants and permission to get that kind of access."

"It's not like it hasn't been done without a warrant before," I grumbled.

"I don't understand you," Samuel said. "You want to insult the NOPD all day long, but then you complain to me that you need things from them every chance you get."

We fell silent for a while. The tension heavy between us.

"You're getting me those reports tomorrow," I said softly.

"What?"

"You told me you'd get them the next time you worked," I pressed. "And you work tomorrow."

"Yeah," Samuel said. "Tomorrow."

"With the Georgianos butting their noses into the case, I'm afraid we're more behind than I'd like."

"Didn't he tell you that the case was yours?"

I barked out a harsh laugh. "I don't believe that for one second. Franklin is a politician at his core, he'll say anything to anyone to put them at ease."

The lines of the road blurred before my eyes, and I blinked hard. "I highly doubt we've seen the last of the Georgianos on this case."

"Thank you, though," I said after a moment. "For stopping him in the hallway, I mean."

"Anytime," Samuel said. I felt his eyes on me as I drove.

I smiled. I didn't hate having him at my side. Even if he wouldn't make police reports magically appear out of thin air.

I pulled onto the highway heading north again, back to New Orleans. Back toward home. "I think the Bettencourts lied to me about when they last saw Mr. Peter Grassi," I said. "I want to know why."

"Of course," Samuel said.

"We still don't know if she was taken or if she left voluntarily," I said.

"That's true."

"I had hoped Mr. Grassi would be a slam dunk. From his mug shot, he looked perfectly capable of participating in a kidnapping, but the man we just spoke to looked like a well-bred businessman."

"Looks can be deceiving," Samuel said. "There's plenty of well-bred men who end up being monsters."

An image of Richard Bettencourt flashed unbidden through my mind.

"It is odd that the cameras around their home were broken the night their daughter went missing," Samuel mused.

"Could just be bad luck," I said.

"There are very few coincidences that aren't worth asking about."

"Mm," I said. "I suppose I should be paying the Bettencourts another in-person visit."

"That may be prudent."

I didn't laugh at his use of the word prudent. Incredible restraint if you ask me. "You want to come too?"

"Mansion row? Rich people with servants and big houses and fancy cars?" he looked down at his immaculate clothing, his designer loafers. "I guess I could tag along."

I laughed. "Okay, but we need food first. I'm starving."

---

I called the Bettencourt home from the small burger shack where we stopped. Freyja picked up on the second ring.

"I'm sorry, Miss Haley," she said. "Mr. Bettencourt is out, and Mrs. Bettencourt is not feeling well."

Grief does that to a person, I thought.

"Can you ask them to give me a call as soon as they get a chance," I said.

"Of course, Miss Haley."

"And Freyja?"

"Yes, Miss Haley?"

"You can call me anytime," I said. "Whatever you need."

There was a long pause on the phone. An almost impossible silence as only a fae can make. "Yes, Miss Haley."

I hung up the cell phone and tucked back into my burger.

"No luck, huh?" Samuel asked from across the table.

"No," I said. "What time are you off tomorrow? Maybe we should just drop by then."

"Sometime after noon," Samuel said. "It's not a long shift."

I didn't know how shifts worked at the NOPD. Noon sounded like a reasonable amount of time to hold off on visiting the Bettencourts.

"Sounds fine," I said. "Call me when you're off, and I'll come pick you up."

"What are you going to be doing?"

"I'd like to do some more research," I said. "Everyone seems pretty convinced that Lucy wouldn't just up and leave town, but I want to know for myself."

"You're going to dive into the high school girl's inner psyche?"

"It wouldn't be the first time." Understanding other girls was the only way to *survive* high school when I was growing up.

Samuel raised an eyebrow at me. "Good luck with that."

"Thanks," I said. "You're paying for lunch."

"Rookie rules?"

"Nah, you're just the only one of us with a steady income at the moment."

"Ah," Samuel said and pulled out his wallet. "That will teach me."

---

The call woke me at five in the morning. I rubbed the sleep from my eyes and stared at the glare of the phone screen. Unrecognized number.

I answered. "This is Meranda."

"Meranda?" I recognized Jill Logan's voice on the other end of the phone. The strain in the secretary's tone told me she was anxious about something. "We need you to come down to the Academy. Quickly, please."

I was already vertical and pulling a pair of dark wash jeans on as I asked, "What's going on?"

"It's about Lucy Bettencourt," Jill said. "I don't know how it ended up here, but you'd better come quickly."

It was pure luck that I had driven the Agency car home the night before. I took half a minute to finish dressing and left my small house, calling a quick see-you-later to the ghost who hadn't shown herself yet this morning.

There was no swarm of police vehicles outside of Crescent City Academy when I arrived. I had half expected the place to be crawling with uniformed officers by the panicked tones I had picked up in the Jill's voice. I stalked through the rose garden and up the paved pathway to the front entrance to the main hall. The sun had yet to grace the horizon at this time of the morning. Not even a glow made its way to this deserted path. I pulled my dark leather jacket closer around my frame.

The main entrance doors were locked tight, and I

rapped on the French windows. A man I didn't recognize in a maintenance uniform let me in. I blinked into the harsh lights of the main hall. Before I could ask where Jill was, the sound of her low heels clomping against the polished wood floor alerted me to her hasty advance.

"Thank you for coming so early, I'm sorry to have called you out of bed." The strain remained in her tone, but her face held only a neutrally pleasant expression.

"This way," she said. She turned on her heel and led me up the hall. The darkness outside caused the glass to only display our reflections as we passed up the French window lined hall. I suppressed the urge to pull my jacket tighter again. Honestly, why was this place so creepy in the dark?

I pulled my gaze away from the darkened windows as Geoff Harnock came into view. His daughter stood beside him a scowl fixed on her face. Judging by the workout gear and sheen of sweat on her upper lip, the master-at-arms had gotten her up far earlier than I would have liked at that age either.

"Master Harnock," I said. "Artemis."

Artemis gave me a look that only sixteen-year-olds can conjure and turned to glare out the windows. Joke's on her; all she could see there was her own ugly expression. Maybe that'd make her school her face right.

"Meranda," Geoff Harnock's voice rumbled to me. "Thank you for coming. I didn't know if we should call the police yet or—"

I planted my boots firmly on the floor, sure that I wasn't going to like the answer to my next question. "What is it?"

Jill Logan made a small sound beside me and gestured to the cork board that occupied five feet of the middle of the hall. I took a step toward it and stopped short. On any given day, this board with covered with different colored fliers and announcements for upcoming events. Mostly student run, it was a conglomeration of band show invites and upcoming dance propaganda. But today, the entire surface of the board was covered in black and white photos. Nearly two dozen of them, all the same, overlapping one another.

My mouth went dry as I stared into the wide eyes of the girl in the photograph. A strip of cloth covered her mouth, tied tightly enough to imprint her cheeks. Mascara had run down her face, smudging about her eyes, and giving her a hollow, haunted appearance. Not much could be seen below her shoulder line, but I could tell that whatever fabric she had been wearing had been ripped down her chest. It wasn't enough skin to be called explicit, but suggestive perhaps. I'd seen enough smiling school photos of the girl to know, it was Lucy Bettencourt.

Words were printed on the bottom border of the page. I studied them: Fifteen million dollars in unmarked cash. Behind Crescent City Academy gymnasium. By Tuesday morning. If you ever want to see Lucy alive again.

The sentences were placed oddly. The whole text read jerkily, like it had been written by a machine that was just learning what English sentence structure was.

I squinted at the photo again. There was something strangely familiar about the whole thing. The pose, the torn shirt, the smudged make-up. Hell, even the way her brown hair framed her face, almost as though it had been freshly curled and hair sprayed into compliance.

"Should we call the police?" Jill asked.

"Not yet," I said. My words were slow as my mind worked overtime, trying to figure out where I'd seen this picture before. "Surely you have security cameras here overnight? Was anyone here yesterday who can confirm if these pictures were up yet?"

"Burt was here," Jill said. She beckoned to the maintenance worker who had let me in.

"Miss Logan," he said. His drawl reminded me of Joseph.

"Were these photos here yesterday when you were working?"

"No ma'am," Burt said. His eyes were wide and sincere.

I nodded once. "Security cameras?"

"In the Dean's office," Jill said. "We can view the footage there."

"Miss Logan," Burt said again. "Do you want me to take these down. Y'know, afore the students arrive?"

Jill pressed a hand to her forehead and looked at me. I surveyed the photos once more. The pieces of the puzzle were starting to click into place. This didn't strike me as the work of an actual kidnapper. Why would he choose to break into a school to deliver a ransom note? The school wasn't going to be the one paying.

I gave the poster another long look. I *had* seen this pose before. At the end of the last school year, one of those two cent vamp bands had released an album. The album cover was this exact pose. Some innocent-looking, thin brunette, bound and gagged. The sort of picture that made rebellious teens want to buy their music and hide it from their parents. I'd seen plenty of the students of Crescent City Academy attempting to recreate that cover themselves.

I was sure this photo had been taken long before Lucy Bettencourt disappeared. Judging by the number of followers I had seen on her internet profile, if she'd posted her rendition of the cover, any number of her fellow students could have found the picture and saved it to their computer. I was almost certain this wasn't a part of Lucy's disappearance.

"Take them down," I said. "And check the rest of the school. This may not be the only place these were posted."

Master Harnock made a disapproving sound beside me.

I looked at him. His granite face was harder still, the sun-wrought lines appearing deeper as he scowled at the board. So that's where his daughter got that look.

"I don't like it," he said.

"A girl is missing, Master Harnock," I said. "Nothing about this is likable."

I followed Jill to the Dean's office, grateful that the students wouldn't be arriving for another hour or so. Crescent City Academy had a high-tech enough security system that we could fast forward on the footage to see what we were looking for. Not just the grounds, but the hallways themselves had cameras set up. It wasn't that fights were common at such an elite academy, but it was standard of practice at this point for any school. Parents expected their chosen institution to be able to keep an eye on their child.

Jill perched on the front of the Dean's high-backed leather chair and ran through the footage. I stood beside her, keeping enough distance between myself and her green cardigan that the cat hair wouldn't send me into a sneezing fit.

"Here," Jill said. She paused the footage and tapped on the screen.

I leaned in. A slight figure in a dark hoodie could be seen entering the Academy. The face was obscured by the hood in this frame, but we kept watching. Jill switched video feeds to track the individual's movement through the school hall. We watched the hooded figure approach the announcement board in the middle of the hall and unsling a satchel that had been obscured by their body. I squinted. I knew that satchel. I had just seen it.

No face could be seen as the figure removed supplies from the satchel and stapled sheet after sheet of Lucy Bettencourt's face onto the board. Once the entire board was covered, the figure turned and moved quickly back up the hall. The face was obscured throughout the entire incident. It was almost as if the perpetrator knew the school well and knew where every camera had been placed on the hall. That only served to confirm my suspicions. I knew who this was.

Jill rewound the footage to watch it again, but I straightened. It would do no good. If this was who I suspected, she wouldn't let her face be seen. Taking a recognizable satchel though, that was interesting. Perhaps a part of her wanted to be caught. Maybe that's what this was all about.

"I'm going to go check on the clean-up," I said, stepping away from the desk.

Jill waved me out the door without taking her eyes off the screen. Her pupils practically glowed in the reflection.

The main hall was empty, the announcement board clear as I passed. I took a right at the end of the hall and moved quickly toward the gym. I'd imagine that's where my culprit would be. Working out with her father.

---

Crescent City Academy's Gymnasium smelled of rubber soles and some kind of sanitizer that made my nose burn. I was just thankful it covered the unwashed socks smell that had been here before the weekend and the deep cleaning crew had had their way. The sound of tennis shoes squeaking on the basketball floor drew me forward. I rounded the bleachers and paused to take in the scene before me.

Geoff Harnock, ranger from the west, master-at-arms for Crescent City Academy, sparred with his daughter. He held padded mitts up to just above his jawline and I watched as he darted his left hand out in a strike toward the sixteen-year-old before him. Artemis was a blur, ducking below the swipe and responding with a punch of her own, directed toward the left of her father's jaw, where he was momentarily exposed. Master Harnock pulled his chin back and out of reach of her strike with almost preternatural speed. The benefits of a life spent fighting in the wildlands between cities.

I expected them to break apart. A moment to catch their breath, maybe. But Artemis pressed her advantage. As her father was off balance from the dodge, she dropped to the floor and flung a leg out to sweep his feet out from under him. In a move that I had been certain was only possible in movies, Geoff Harnock marked his daughter's intention and sprang into the air at the last second. A spectacular back bending handspring followed, and I took the opportunity to clap as he stuck the landing.

Both Harnocks turned toward the sound of my applause. Artemis' chest was heaving as she worked to catch her breath, but her father was the picture of rested ease.

"Ms. Haley," he said. "You want to join in the lesson?"

Artemis scowled behind his shoulder. Something told me, as much as she didn't want to be here, she'd like it even less if she had to share this time with another.

I gave a generous chuckle. "No, Master Harnock," I said. "I don't think I could keep up."

The master-at-arms gave me a shrug. He removed one

mitt and scrubbed a finger across his right eye. "Suit yourself."

"I came to let you know that we caught the person who posted the ransom on the security feeds," I said.

I watched Artemis out of the corner of my eye, my senses heightened for any kind of reaction to my words. She didn't give me any visible response, but her scent changed. Uncertainty or fear permeated the room at my words. A sharp smell beneath the notes of sweat and sanitizer.

"Who was it?" Master Harnock's question was a growl.

"We're not sure," I said. "Their face was hidden from the cameras."

Artemis had kept her face neutral when I had spoken at first, but now I could see an ease of tension in her shoulders, her jawline.

"Are we giving the footage to the police?" Master Harnock asked.

"That's up to the Dean," I said.

Harnock grunted. I couldn't tell if it was a sign of approval or disapproval. He rubbed his eye again.

"You alright there?" I asked.

Artemis cast a glance at her father's back, her brows drawn together. To my surprise, she raised a hand toward him. It was a half attempt at affection and comfort.

"Damn new contacts," Harnock said. "They're just irritating."

I nodded. Artemis' hand fell. I wondered how many times she had pursued affection from her father and had it turned away in favor of granite and the hardness he thought she needed more.

"Are you sure you don't want to train?" Geoff Harnock asked. He fixed his eyes on me. The white of his right eye was beginning to redden from his ministrations.

"I'm okay," I said.

"If you change your mind," the master-at-arms said, "you know where to find me. I'm sure it would be helpful to have some practice seeing as you're working the street again."

"It's just the one case," I said.

"Suit yourself," Harnock said.

I cast a look toward the pile of workout gear. "Nice satchel," I said.

Artemis' eyes widened for a split second before she schooled herself. "Thanks."

I could confront her here, in front of her father. I could tell them both that I knew she'd been the one to break into the school and put up those ransom posters. But I didn't.

If her reasons for doing it were anything near what I suspected, it would only be cruel to call her out here in front of him. It was his attention that she wanted. I wouldn't give her the negative interaction she sought. I'd talk to Master Harnock later. Encourage him to give his daughter what she really needed. Not more combat lessons. Not more early wakings. Maybe just a night in with a movie. Maybe just a drive to get ice cream. Daughters needed love from their fathers. I knew that as well as anyone.

I left the gym before my thoughts could turn any more nostalgic. Now was not the time to dwell on my relationship with my father. There was work to do.

# Chapter Ten

I grimaced at the sight of the building before me. New Orleans Police Department's Eighth Precinct truly was a sight to behold. Somewhere in the far distant past, long before portals started opening and the humans had to make architectural choices around the brave new world that was forming around them, someone had *chosen* to design the gaudiest building in the city and give it to the NOPD. An awful, creamed peach color occupied the outside of the building on any wall surface that wasn't taken up by squat round columns. White columns weren't a new architectural choice in New Orleans and plenty of houses and businesses sported them well, but the rotund nature of the columns before me only served to make the precinct look squat. Haphazard and ugly.

I forced down my feelings of revulsion as I crossed through the front doors to the building. I had heard the stories of men and women being dragged into this precinct; charges filed against them for crimes that they didn't commit. Plenty of were-creatures had been falsely accused in the last few decades, the police detectives just looking for a higher percentage of closed cases, not necessarily looking for the right guy.

A reporter, Leslie Hagen, had recently been publishing investigative articles on such cases. The police had sworn, as political pressure was applied, that they were changing their ways. That they would be better from now on. I didn't hold my breath. I wouldn't even be here if I didn't have to get those evidence reports from Sammy. He'd promised me that he'd have them today and dropping in on him may be rude, but I'd spent enough time researching on my own to realize I needed them.

After the early morning call to the school, I'd spent the rest of the morning reviewing Lucy Bettencourt's internet presence. I'd found the image that had been used on the ransom poster. Lucy Bettencourt had posted it at the beginning of the summer to the deafening sound of likes and comments from all her followers.

Looking into the secret lives of the New Orleans teenager had been mostly mind numbing. Rumors and gossip and feuding were vaguely nauseating to me on a good day but add in the melodrama that is every teenage existential crisis, I needed a break. Thankfully, the NOPD precinct where Samuel worked wasn't far away.

The lobby of the precinct was roped in half, the only path to the main counter was guarded by two tall metal detectors with a few rookie officers manning them. I grumbled under my breath about the knife that I would have to hand over to them to be allowed to pass. Everyone in this city carried a weapon of some sort. The fact that they were confiscating the only defense some in this city had upon entry with no indication that the citizen would get their property back made me fume.

The walls seemed to be growing closer as I approached

the officers. I could just imagine myself being carted through this lobby with my hands clasped behind my back if the truth ever came out about what I was. Who my parents really were. Honestly, they may not even bother to bring me to the station, opting for some kind of in-field execution if they deemed me a serious enough threat.

I pushed the thought away and gave the uniformed man on the right what I hoped was an I'm-no-threat-please-don't-shoot-me smile. "Good morning," I greeted him. It was almost eleven thirty. It barely counted as morning, but I wasn't about to say, good noon.

"Ma'am," the officer touched a hand to the bill of his hat. Gotta love that southern hospitality. I checked the name plate across the chest from his NOPD badge: Savron

"I have a four-inch blade in my right boot," I told the officer, my voice matter of fact.

Officer Savron didn't even blink. He pulled a small plastic bin from beneath a metal table to his right. "You may place any metal in the bin."

"Will I get it back?"

"Weapons stay on this side of the rope."

Uh-huh. Not a chance then.

I gave him another smile and drew the blade out slowly. I transferred it to my left hand, holding the blade by the flat side between my thumb and forefinger so the policeman could see I wasn't about to use it. I placed it gently into the bin along with my cell phone and keys. I slipped my satchel from my side, placed it on the table and patted the pockets of my black jeans to show him that they were empty.

"Go ahead on through," Officer Savron directed.

I stepped through the detector, relieved that it didn't alarm even though I knew my pockets were empty.

Another officer met me on the other side, and Officer

Savron handed him the bin of my belongings, sans knife, of course. The new officer, DuCott, sported a thick blond mustache and heavy brows. He appeared to be nearing middle age. *Probably not a rookie*, I thought.

"Step right over here, ma'am," Officer DuCott directed.

I saw that the table behind him held a small clear plastic bottle complete with a spray nozzle. Ah, mer-checks. They really are getting worried. Whatever was happening in the Gulf, it had to be something big. I really needed to watch the news more.

"Sorry about this." He sounded like he meant it. I gave the older officer a what-can-you-do shrug of sympathy, then held myself still, closing my eyes against what was to come. Standing in this manner, this vulnerable, unarmed at that, my mind was screaming at me to run. Shut up, I told it. The spray came, a strange itching sensation and I could smell the salt that they had added to the concentration. Not for the first time, I was grateful I had invested in waterproof mascara.

I opened my eyes and blinked once. Officer DuCott held out a white washcloth, and took it gratefully and patted my face dry. I handed the cloth back and DuCott passed me the plastic bin. I picked my phone and keys out of it, shoving them into my pockets and slinging my satchel back over my shoulder.

"Have a nice day, ma'am."

"Thanks." I could still taste the salt on my tongue. I wished for some water to wash it away. Damn, I hated when humans got nervous.

The police precinct's front counter was manned by a bored looking woman who was scribbling on a piece of newspaper with a pencil. Crossword, I guessed. She wore glasses attached to a beaded necklace, and I wondered if I wanted someone working for the NOPD who had to keep her glasses on a leash in order to find them. Her hair was curled close to her head like a fluffy brunette helmet, and her nails, though kept short, were painted a light shade of pink.

"How can I help you?" Her voice had a slight drawl to it as though she had been raised outside of the city, someplace referred to as the deep south.

"I am looking for Officer LaMontagne," I said. I leaned my elbows on the counter, peeking behind it by force of habit. Not a crossword, I saw. Sudoku.

The woman blinked at me twice as though it took a moment for her to process my words, then with a massive sigh, as though I had asked her to climb four flights of stairs to fetch me a soda, she turned to her computer and began typing.

After what seemed like an eternity of her typing and scrolling and never once looking up at me, she said, "We don't seem to have anyone here by that name."

What the hell? "Can you check again?"

"Are you sure you have the right precinct?" Her voice was saccharine, but the look she gave me told me that she thought I was a simpleton.

"Yes," I snapped. "I'm sure. Are you sure you spelled it right?"

The woman looked aghast that I would suggest such an insult against her vast intelligence. I leaned into it to spite her. "It's capital L-A capital M-O-N—"

"I know how to spell LaMontagne," the woman hissed. "I am telling you he does not work here. Now may I direct you to another officer you can speak to about your—" she looked me up and down. "—problems."

Now it was my turn to look aghast. She thought I was a

confidential informant. As though I'd be dumb enough to play snitch in *this* city.

"Forget it," I said.

"Excuse me," Officer DuCott called my attention across the room.

I turned to him.

"You talking about Samuel LaMontagne?"

"Yes!" I gave the woman behind the counter an ugly look and walked back toward the metal detectors.

When I was close enough that only I could hear what he said, DuCott spoke again. "I wouldn't say his name too loudly in here."

I felt my brow crinkle. "What do you mean?"

"He didn't leave on good terms."

I shook my head. "Leave? No, he still works here."

"Ma'am, Samuel LaMontagne hasn't worked here in almost two years."

A ball of unease settled in the pit of my stomach. "That can't be right. He would have told me—" I paused. Would he have? We hadn't seen each other in years, would he have sought me out just to tell me he left his job? And I had sat there demanding he get evidence reports and witness statements and he—

Dammit, why didn't he say something?

I schooled my face into a neutral expression. "Thank you, officer."

I turned to leave. My legs were almost numb as I made my way back across the lobby.

Now it made sense why he'd been drunk in the middle of the afternoon on Friday. Why he'd had the time to work so closely with my father for the last year. Why he wanted to take the Agency off my hands. He didn't have anything else.

I pushed my way out the front door and into the bright sunshine. I had to call him, and neither of us were going to like it.

---

Samuel picked up the phone after the first ring. "Hello?"

"Hey Sammy, you have those evidence reports yet?" I paced on the sidewalk in front of the precinct.

"No— uh— not yet. I'm working on it."

"Oh, well maybe I should come in and help you find them. I'm right outside your building."

"You're outside?"

I almost smiled at the horror in his voice.

"New Orleans Police Department, Precinct Eight. Hideous orange building. I could just pop right in."

"No, don't go in." He sounded breathless. "I'm not even there right now."

"Oh, you aren't?" I poured every ounce of innocence I could muster into my voice. "Are you out doing important *police* work, Sammy? Are you working with the *police* on a case?"

There was a pause on his end. "You know."

"What the hell, Sammy?"

"I know. I should have told you."

I pushed down the sharp pang that hit my heart. "It's been almost two years."

"I should have told you right away, but I just couldn't. And then time had passed, and we hadn't seen each other in a while anyway. What was I supposed to do when you called? Open with a 'hey Mer, a bunch of people died, and they fired me a couple years ago, how's the teaching job going?' Come on."

A bunch of people died? Oh, we were definitely going to talk about that.

"Where are you?" I asked.

"I'm at home."

"Send me your address," I hung up the phone.

A second later the text message blinked through. I set off for a streetcar.

---

Samuel opened the door as I raised my hand to knock, almost as though he had been waiting for me. He looked terrible. He kept his hair buzzed too short for me to call it unkempt, but I'm sure it would be if given the chance. Dark circles puffed out under his brown eyes. He wore a wrinkled, white t-shirt, and black sweatpants that had a hole in one knee. As he opened the door wider for me to pass through, he seemed shorter than he'd been yesterday.

"Can I get you a water or tea, maybe?" he asked. I didn't want a drink; I wanted answers.

"What happened, Samuel."

He winced at his full name and sat down hard in a white leather armchair.

"I don't know what you want to hear."

I could've screamed, but I kept my voice steady. "The truth. Just tell me the truth."

A line deepened at the corner of his mouth, and his jaw seemed to tremble. "I don't know where to start."

I sat on the couch facing him, our knees almost touching. We were so close I could feel the heat coming off his body. I wanted nothing more than to wrap my arms around him and make that devastated look on his face go away. But

I couldn't do that. Not yet. Not without knowing what had happened.

"You haven't worked with the NOPD for almost two years. What happened to make you leave?"

Samuel pressed his palms into his eyes so firmly, I could've sworn it hurt.

"We were working a case of smuggling," he began. "Some wannabe pirates from the Gulf were transporting items from the Caribbean. It should have been simple. We'd found out which storehouse the bad guys were using to move illegal goods from the waterfront into the city. Open and shut, all the incriminating evidence should have been in there, you know?"

I nodded.

"I was on a six-man team. We'd been briefed. We all knew what we were supposed to do. I'd worked with these guys plenty of times before. We were like a family," his voice cracked, and he shook his head like a dog shaking water out of its ears. "They either knew we were coming, or they were just overly zealous. The whole place was set to blow the second we entered.

"The door breach went fine, I had been on the battering ram and the second the door swung open, I stepped back so the ones holding their rifles could get through and clear the building. I saw it out of the corner of my eye. A shimmering veil that ran across the whole building. The second the first man stepped through it—" he extended his fingers in an exploding motion. "—boom."

"Boom?"

"Mage's fire," he clarified. "They must have paid a high price for that kind of a trap. The entire team went up."

He blinked once then his eyes locked onto mine. A dark fierceness lay behind their honeyed center. "Have you ever smelled a burning body, Mer? Not what's left behind in a field or an open space once the wind has dispelled some of it, but a real person burning like a torch in front of you?"

My mouth went dry, and I shook my head.

"It's the worst smell in the world and I was surrounded by five of them."

"And you were outside," I said. "That's why you survived?"

"No," he said. "I was in the thick of it with them. The fire didn't touch me."

The hell? "What do you mean it didn't touch you?"

"I mean, I was in the middle of a firestorm, and I felt nothing. There was heat and the — smell— sure, but I didn't burn. Not even when I tackled the officer closest to me and tried to put the flames out with my jacket. My hands passed right through them. I didn't even singe. And putting out mage's fire— you know."

I did know. Mage's fire didn't go out. It burned until it consumed all the fuel around it, and it was forced to peter into nothingness. I had never heard of *anyone* surviving it.

"What did you do?" I asked, my voice a whisper.

"I watched," he squeezed his eyes shut and a tear leaked out. It shimmered in the light as it trailed down his dark cheek. "I called it in on the radio, and I watched as every member of that team burned into bones and ash and the evidence was consumed around them.

"When help arrived, all they could do was dig a trench around the building, wide enough that the mage's fire couldn't cross it. People were gagging on scene from the smell. Some had to put on masks to avoid smoke inhalation and I felt nothing. The medics looked me over and said I was completely unharmed, just a few scrapes and bruises from tackling my buddy and hitting the ground."

"Sammy I—" the words wouldn't come. What was I supposed to say?

Samuel drug a hand down his face. "After that, I was a pariah. No one knew how I'd survived. Hell, *I* didn't know how I'd survived. They tried to float me to different units, but I never really fit in. It made everyone uncomfortable to have me around them, as though *I* was the black cloud that had caused my friends to die."

"That's terrible," I whispered.

Samuel took a deep breath and sat back in his chair. "It is what it is. I can't say I wouldn't have felt the same if I was in their shoes. I left a few months later. They tried to get me to see a department shrink, but she didn't know what to do with me either. She tried, I'll give her that, but one session, I reached across the table for the water pitcher, and she flinched. She actually flinched, Mer. Don't they teach them not to do that sort of thing?"

"Either way," Samuel continued. "I left. Grand-mère talked to your father and a week later he offered me a job working for him."

That made sense. Dad was always picking up the broken things and the lost causes. The mirror held Exhibit A.

"That's why you were drinking in the middle of the day the first time I called?"

"No," Samuel laughed. "I was drinking in the middle of the day because it's fun. We're still in our twenties, Mer. You've gotta live a little."

His voice was sobered when he spoke again. "I've done my best to deal with what I saw that day. Your dad helped a lot."

That also didn't surprise me. Dad had a way of making

the confusing parts of life make more sense. Maybe Florentina was right, maybe I should call him.

"So, no evidence reports then?" I asked, hoping he picked up my jesting tone.

Samuel laughed sharply. "No, no evidence reports. If I could get someone at the station to even *talk* to me, I'm still not sure it would be possible."

"Hell," I said. "There goes your usefulness."

"Hey, I can still play guard dog with the best of them."

Whatever retort I had been preparing was cut off by my phone ringing. I stood and pulled it out of my pocket, pacing to the corner of the room.

"Hello?"

"Miss Haley?" I recognized the soft voice, the lilt.

"Freyja, what's going on?"

"You need to come over, quick. Mr. and Mrs. Bettencourt just received a note. A ransom note."

"I'll be right there."

I hung up the phone and shoved it back in my pocket. "How fast can you change?"

Samuel was already halfway to his bedroom. "Pretty fast, where are we going?"

I saw his shirt half pulled over his head before he left the room, the side of his dark body hardened with muscle that I was sure wasn't caused by sitting around all day.

"The Bettencourts. They got a ransom demand."

"Shit."

"Yeah," I said. "Shit."

A buzz enveloped the Bettencourt's house when we arrived. Two NOPD squad cars and one unmarked police car sat on the gravel of the driveway. With all the activity, the front door had been left open, so Samuel and I walked in. Freyja looked up from a side table she had been dusting and nodded her head toward the parlor where I had first met the Bettencourts. I murmured my thanks, and Samuel and I let ourselves into the room, lingering near the wall to observe what was happening.

Four uniformed officers busied themselves as only worker bees can. A mass of technological equipment, all wires and speakers and earbuds, was spread across the low table of the parlor. A black handset and base of a landline sat in the middle of it all.

Louisa Bettencourt sat on the pink chaise, the picture of poise in grief. Her legs were crossed at the ankle, the left one tucked behind the right. Her black pencil skirt was smoothed to her knees and her silk top the color of cream was unwrinkled. But the mascara around her eyes was smudged, and her hands gripped a handkerchief in her lap, squeezing at it like a stress ball.

Mr. Bettencourt was on his feet behind her, a hand on her shoulder, a protective posture or maybe possessive. His white dress shirt was tucked into his black slacks separated only by a dark leather belt that I was sure matched his shoes.

Neither of the Bettencourts looked up when we snuck into the room, their attention wrapped up by the man and woman in cheap suits who were talking to them. NOPD detectives. Great.

"Walk me through it again," the detective on the left was saying. "You got up this morning, stepped out onto your front porch, and found the picture there?"

"No, I told you already," Richard Bettencourt said. It seemed to me that this wasn't the first time they'd had him reiterate the story. "Freda found it when she came in this morning and it wasn't a picture, it was a flash drive."

"And you waited to call us until you had opened the file and printed it?"

The detective's voice was harsh, accusatory. I saw Mrs. Bettencourt close her eyes against it. Freyja was right, she looked terrible. All long lines and baggy eyes that were barely covered over with foundation.

Mr. Bettencourts grip seemed to tighten on the back of the sofa. "No, I had Freda call you right away."

"But you put the flash drive into your computer and checked what was on it before we arrived. Mr. Bettencourt, surely you can understand how that makes our job more difficult."

"I wore gloves," Richard Bettencourt snapped. "I'm not an idiot."

"Certainly not," the detective said, his voice sounding as though he wasn't convinced.

"I will not be treated this way in my own home." Mr. Bettencourt seemed to gain a few inches of height as his indignation forced his spine straight. "I have given *thousands* to the police department, and you come in here with accusations against a grieving father! Who would you like to accuse next, perhaps Louisa hasn't been through enough already!"

Louisa made a strangled sob and pressed the handkerchief to her face.

The second detective rose then. A woman in a tan suit. "Mr. Bettencourt, I'm sure detective Roth meant no offense. Roth, go to the car."

The first detective scowled but spun on his heel and left without further protest.

Ah, the power of money and well-placed donations.

The mere threat of reduced funding for the department was enough to change the investigatory trajectory. This is why the humans thought they were untouchable.

Richard Bettencourt met my gaze then, seeming to just notice we'd arrived. "Ms. Haley, thank you for coming."

"Of course," I said, crossing the room. "This is Sam, he's assisting in the investigation."

The NOPD detective rose at the sound of my voice and turned. She was middle aged with hard ice blue eyes. Her blond hair was pulled tightly into a bun at the nape of her neck, not a hair out of place.

I stuck out a hand to the woman. "Meranda Haley, Collier Investigations."

"Detective Hill," she said. Her eyebrows rose as she shook my hand. I could tell she was surprised by my presence, but not impressed. Most police detectives weren't when a PI was stepping all over their investigation.

"Freyja found the flash drive," I said, trying to steer the conversation before the detective could take it over. "Was it in an envelope or lying on the doorstep?"

"No envelope," Mr. Bettencourt said. "It was taped to the front door when she arrived."

"What time did she come in this morning?"

"She had most of the morning off, maybe closer to noon."

"Did she pull the drive off the door, or did she call you and you took it."

"I took it, she didn't touch it."

One set of prints other than what we were looking for, then.

"Are your cameras fixed yet, Mr. Bettencourt?" I asked.

Richard Bettencourt seemed to deflate. "I—had other things on my mind."

"Understandable," I said. "May I see the image that was on the flash drive?"

Another sob from Mrs. Bettencourt as one of the uniformed officers passed me a printout. The photo was grainy as though it had been taken on a crap camera in a dull light. One figure, Lucy, tied to a chair. Her brown hair flopped over her brow, obscuring the left side of her face. A scrap of cloth was tied across her mouth, her nose peeking out above it. It was uncannily similar to the posters that had been taped up at the school. I hated it.

Lucy's hands were behind her back, but a newspaper had been propped on her lap, leaning against her chest. Today's headline. She was still alive.

"Was there any text with the photo?" Samuel asked, peering over my shoulder at the picture.

"Just instructions to wait for a phone call, not to leave home, and not to call the police." Mr. Bettencourt said.

"Which you didn't obey?" Samuel asked.

"The police were already involved," Mr. Bettencourt said. "If the kidnappers didn't know that, they can't be watching us too closely. It's a bluff."

He sounded awfully sure of that. Too many crime shows and not enough police reports were consumed in this house, I thought.

"You did the right thing," Detective Hill assured him.

I pulled Samuel to the side of the room, out of the detective's earshot.

"Go to the car, there's a duffle in the back that should have everything you need. Walk down the street in both directions. Any house that has a camera pointed at the street, ask to see their footage for last night and this morning. You should be able to copy it over to our own drive in no time, and we can review it later."

I passed a Collier Investigations card into his hands. "If anyone gives you trouble, show them this. It's not a badge, but not everyone cares enough to stop you if you show them some kind of identification."

Samuel nodded curtly and left without question. I could get used to having a partner who didn't talk back, I thought.

Detective Hill was speaking when I returned to the center of the parlor.

"We will be taking the flash drive as evidence of course, but I will be leaving an officer outside. If the call comes through, send someone out for the officer and keep the caller on the line as long as possible. The trace should begin automatically, but the more time you give it, the better."

Mr. Bettencourt nodded. "Thank you, detective."

"We'll find her, Mr. Bettencourt. I know it doesn't feel like it, but the ransom demand is good news," Detective Hill said.

I cast my eyes on Mrs. Bettencourt. She didn't react to the detective's words. Her gaze was fixed on a spot on the carpet, glazing over. She looked like she needed to be in bed with a blanket pulled up to her chin, not sitting on a chaise with a pencil skirt and makeup on.

Mr. Bettencourt looked to me as Detective Hill left the room, the rest of the officers trailing after her, leaving behind their equipment. "Anything else I can tell you, Ms. Haley?"

I sat on the couch that the detective had vacated. "I just want to confirm a few things. When I called a few days ago, Mrs. Bettencourt said that you hadn't seen Peter Grassi in years. Is that true?"

"Yes, I believe he came over for Christmas a few years back."

I nodded. So, either he or Mr. Grassi was lying.

"Mrs. Bettencourt," I said.

She turned those glassy eyes to me. I was sure she was somewhere behind them, but I couldn't see any kind of a spark, a fight.

"Get some rest," I said. "We can only wait for the call now. Lucy will need you to be well when she comes home."

Mrs. Bettencourt squeezed her eyes shut and a tear fell leaving a trail down the powder on her cheek.

"Freda," Mr. Bettencourt called. The fae appeared in the doorway. "Get Mrs. Bettencourt to bed, please. Give her some of that medicine Dr. Gallo prescribed."

"She hasn't been sleeping well," he explained to me. "Our family doctor was kind enough to get us something to help."

I nodded. If it was my kid, I wouldn't sleep either.

I watched as Freyja navigated Louisa out of the room with an arm around her waist. "Mr. Bettencourt," I said. "Is there anything else you want to tell me."

It was a chance. Usually, people with something to hide didn't come right out and tell based on juvenile questions, but it was worth a shot. Mr. Bettencourt shook his head, but I scented something on the air. Fear. Raw and human.

I rose from the couch. "Please call me if anything comes up." I nodded toward the phone. "Or if a call comes through."

Mr. Bettencourt nodded and sank down onto the chaise his wife had left. As I walked from the room, I saw him lean forward and put his forehead in his hands.

I met Samuel on the street. He hadn't gotten footage from every house, but at least one coming from each side of the Bettencourt's address had given us something. We drove back to the Agency.

"Did they say anything else after I left?" Samuel asked.

"The police took the flash drive with them, of course. I would have liked to see the prints but…"

"Yeah."

"Mr. Bettencourt is hiding something."

"You think so?"

"I asked him point blank about seeing Peter Grassi. He assured me it had been years. Someone's lying." I didn't tell him about the fear in Richard Bettencourt's scent. He wouldn't understand.

"Well, let's order in some food and review the footage. There has to be something worth seeing on those tapes."

I nodded. Assuming someone hadn't glamoured themselves against being picked up on video, I thought. The humans probably wouldn't know how to do that, but certainly with enough money passing hands, someone could make it happen.

# Chapter Eleven

Florentina had just finished a reading when we arrived at the Agency. A spooked-looking man pushed his way out the door as we entered, in a hurry to put distance between himself and the building.

"Geez Tante," I said. "You sure know how to let 'em down easy."

My aunt stood in the curtained doorway to her Parlor and thumbed through a stack of dollar bills before hiding them away in her wide yellow skirts. "He has been cheating on his wife for the last month and a half. I told him she knew, and she was taking all of his assets with her."

I raised an eyebrow. "It was the truth?"

"It was *a* truth," Florentina said, a wicked twinkle in her eye.

Samuel let out a low chuckle and leaned in to kiss his grandmother's cheek.

"You have work to do?" Florentina asked.

"A ransom came in," Samuel said. "I have footage to review."

He and the duffle bag disappeared into my father's office.

When it was just my aunt and me in the hall, she spoke again. "Have you spoken with your father?"

"Not yet."

"He misses you."

"He told you that?" I asked, trying to keep the bemusement out of my voice.

"Not in so many words," Florentina said. "But yes."

The silence stretched.

"He can help you with the case."

"Like he helped me by giving me this Agency in the first place?" I asked, "Saddling me with so much debt that I can never get rid of the thing?"

"You're upset."

"What gave it away, Tante?" I asked. That wasn't fair, but I couldn't stop now. "I had planned on handing Collier Investigations over to your grandson, but without a steady income, that kind of debt? It would be a curse."

"He told you about leaving the police department."

"It took a while, but yeah."

"Your dad was a help to him during that time."

"He mentioned that."

"He could help you too."

"Drop it, Tante," I said.

Florentina put her hands up. "I do not wish to fight with you, girl. But I know you."

I tried not to roll my eyes. Sometimes Florentina had a way of making me feel exactly as I had at sixteen, when all the adults were impossible, and if only I was in charge, everything would be turning up aces.

"You will let your pride eat you up until there is nothing left."

Her words were a punch to my gut, taking the wind out of me.

"You are too stubborn to admit that you are *afraid*."

I winced.

"You pretend you can ignore the spirits, so you never have to deal with them," she continued. "You pretend you can ignore the gaping hole your father left in your heart. But you can't. And the more you try, the more this pride will consume you and you will be of no help to anyone."

"Okay, ouch," I said. "Enough."

"You need to learn to deal with your powers. You need to learn to handle the ghosts and defend against them before they get out of hand, but more than that—," Florentina softened her voice. "You need to talk to your father. There are truths you both need to hear."

"I—"

"The next words out of your mouth ought to be, 'yes, Tante', or 'thank you, Tante'," she said.

I cast my eyes to the ceiling and took a deep breath. She was right. I hated that she was right. The gaping hole in my heart ached that she was right.

"Yes, Tante," I said, finally. "Thank you, Tante."

"Now you go upstairs and call up your father," she said. "I will tell Samuel that you will be right down."

Any protest died on my lips at her curt direction.

The hallway seemed impossibly long as I made my way toward the stairs. The stairs themselves, I could have sworn were steeper than they used to be. I used the banister to pull myself up, my legs getting heavier with each step.

I paused before the door that closed off the upstairs apartment from the staircase itself. I could just stand here for an hour, come back down, and tell Florentina that I'd called him. But she'd know. She always knew when someone lied to her. I bit back the curse I wanted to shout and put the key in the doorknob, twisting it and pushing forward into my father's apartment.

---

It was like he'd never left. Not an item of his familiar apartment was out of place. The green and gray patterned rug that he'd placed in the middle of the living room to cover the scratches the coffee table had made on the hardwood floor. I walked through the living room, past the worn brown couch and into the kitchen. The counters in the kitchen were cleaned and organized, every jar and utensil in its place. The cupboards all closed up tightly save the one above the coffee maker that I had always packed too full of different brands of tea to shut properly. I turned on my heel and walked back into the living room.

The hallway across from the stairs, I didn't explore. I didn't need to. I knew what lay that way. I knew that the bathroom was at the end of the hall and that my bedroom was the last door on the right. I knew he hadn't changed a thing in there since I left. I also knew that his room was across the hall from mine and that it would smell like him. Like pipe tobacco and warmth and safety.

I flopped down on the brown leather couch in the living room and threw my legs up on the coffee table. Sitting here, steeping in these memories, feeling the weight of how much I missed him—I knew my aunt had been right. I had to call him.

"Dad?"

A surprised noise, then, "Hey, kiddo."

I swallowed the lump that immediately rose in response to his deep steady voice. *Dammit, get it together, Meranda.*

"Hey, Dad. H-how are you?"

"Could be better," he said. "Wish I was there with you."

"Me too."

"You got into the Agency, okay?"

"Yeah," I said, remembering the note that he'd left with the key ring telling me that the front door stuck sometimes. "No problems. I'm even working a case."

"Is that so? That's excellent. I knew you'd fall right back into the rhythm."

I wanted to yell. I wanted to tell him that I hadn't wanted to come back. That him giving me this Agency was a dirty trick to get me back into the game. But I couldn't. Not when I heard the pride in his voice that I was on the streets again.

"Samuel's helping me," I said finally.

"Yeah? He's a good kid."

"He is," I paused. "I was gonna give him the Agency."

A sharp intake of breath hit my ears.

"After a while," I said quickly. I hadn't wanted to piss him off. "Once we've worked a couple of cases. Gotten some of the expenses taken care of. Then I could feel good, going back to the Academy and knowing the Agency was in good hands."

The silence that stretched was oppressive. My breath hitched in my throat.

"What's your case?" Dad's voice was gentle. He had to know it was difficult for me to tell him I wanted to give away his gift, just as it was difficult for him to hear it.

"A girl was snatched off Bourbon Street," I said. I summed up the investigation we'd done so far, ending with collecting the surveillance tapes from the Bettencourt's street.

"You have Samuel looking at those now?"

"Yeah."

"That's good. He's the one who should be seeing them."

"What do you mean?"

"He sees things differently. Ask him sometime. He sees things that not everyone can."

That made about as much sense as me being left the Agency, I supposed.

I thought back to the cabin we had found, the address near Manchac that had been falling apart. Samuel had asked why we hadn't gone into it, but from what I could tell, there was no way the entrance would have supported even my weight. Maybe dad was right. I should ask him about it.

"Well, Dad," I said. "I should be getting back to the case."

"Oh." A disappointed sound that stabbed into my heart.

"We'll talk again soon," I said. "I promise."

"I love you, Mer," he said. "Never forget that."

"I know, Dad. I love you too."

At that moment, I wanted nothing more than for him to be there. Really be there, in that room. To wrap his arms around me like he had when I was young and just hold me tightly.

But he wasn't.

And he couldn't.

I made my way back down the stairs to the main level with even heavier steps than I had ascended. A pressure was building in my chest with each step until I was sure I would explode. I had to do something to release this tension. I stepped into the Agency's kitchen and ran my hands under cold water from the faucet. I turned it as cold as possible and stuck my arms under its stream. Further and further up until I was chilled nearly to my armpits. I focused on that water, the goosebumps that traveled across my chest at its touch. My skin seemed to shimmer under its flow as if the cascade was depositing sparkles on my flesh.

Finally, my head cleared. I turned off the faucet, filled a glass of water from the pitcher beside the sink and went to find Samuel.

***

Samuel had a laptop open on the desk beside my father's computer. I recognized it as one of the resources that we had kept in the duffel bag. A sticker with the logo for Collier Investigations adorned its lid from some discount bulk pack dad had bought when we had first started advertising for the Agency.

"Hey," Samuel said, without looking up. "I think we've got something here."

I crossed to him and leaned against the desk as he rewound the video he had been playing. The camera must have been mounted on a gate outside the actual property of whoever's house this was because there was no lawn in the camera's view. It gave a nice picture of the sidewalk and the smooth asphalt of the street beyond. The entirety of the street was visible, all the way across to the opposite property and their brick and wrought iron wall.

"This was from the one house who'd give us footage down the east side of the street. I don't know if whomever dropped off that flash drive knew where the cameras were, but he sure tried hard to stay in the blind spots except for— here!" He tapped a finger against the screen.

I leaned forward. I didn't see anything where his finger had struck. "Show me again?"

He rewound it a few seconds and then played it again. I watched intently where he had pointed the last time.

"There!" He exclaimed. "Did you see it?"

I blinked. I hadn't seen anything.

Samuel made a frustrated noise and muttered something about bats and blindness.

"It's there clear as day."

"What is it you see?" I asked. "Explain it to me as though I *am* part bat."

"For just an instant, between the shadow of the gate there and the tree, there's a man."

I squinted at the screen. There was a shimmering in the air where he pointed, but there definitely wasn't a man.

I couldn't shake the memory of my father's words. *He sees things that not everyone can.*

"Sammy," I said. "What did you see at the cabin?"

Samuel looked at me like I'd grown three heads. "Same thing as you, a cabin."

"Describe it to me."

He hesitated; his brown eyes filled with something akin to trepidation. "It looked like it could use some work. All peeling paint and the window to the left of the door had a crack in it, but nothing that couldn't be fixed."

"The dock? Would you be comfortable tying a boat up there?"

"Sure," Samuel said. "The railings could stand to be replaced, but the structure was sound enough."

I thought of the dock *I* had seen, half disintegrating into the swamp.

"Why are you looking at me like that?"

I forced myself to stop staring. "No reason. You're just—very observant."

Samuel nodded slowly but gave me some serious side-eye as he faced the screen again.

"Can you tell who it is in the video? Do you recognize

them?" I asked.

"I'd have to save a shot from the video and try to increase the size and play with it a bit, but I think I can. It'll take me a minute."

"Go ahead," I said. "I need to talk to Florentina about something real quick."

Samuel waved me away and started typing things on the computer that I couldn't begin to understand.

I made my way across the hall to Florentina's parlor. The heavy curtains were drawn aside, and the room was empty. I pushed through the other side and into the kitchen. Florentina stood at the stove, pouring steaming water from the red tea kettle into a cup.

"Your grandson is a Nullifier," I said, my words an accusation I couldn't temper.

Florentina didn't turn around. She didn't act surprised that I knew. Actually, she never acted surprised by anything, a fact that I found particularly annoying at that moment.

"It took you that long to figure it out?"

Something in me bucked against the derision in her tone.

I clenched and unclenched my teeth.

"You're going to wear your teeth down to nubs if you keep that up."

I rubbed my jaw and scowled at her back. She turned to face me, her wide skirts swishing against the counter. She blew on her tea.

"You're upset."

"Of course, I'm upset," I nearly shouted. "If I'd known what he was, I would have treated this whole investigation differently. There's a girl's life at stake!"

"And if I had told you, would he ever have forgiven

me?" she asked. "Would you if I shared with every stranger I saw what you are, Potesta?" Her Cajun clipped the last word into distinct syllables each punching into my heart with precision.

"That's not fair," I said. "I am hardly a stranger to you."

"No, my dear," my aunt said, settling herself into a chair behind the kitchen table. "But after all the years you've spent apart, to him you are."

I sat heavily on the chair across from her and pressed my palms into my eyes. She was right. I would never have spoken to her again if she had shared my secrets.

"It's how he survived the Mage's Fire."

Florentina nodded and sipped her tea.

"It's how he lived when every member of his team was killed in front of him."

Florentina closed her eyes against the image but nodded again.

"Does he know?" I asked.

Florentina brushed a hand down the front of her white blouse, smoothing it. "I don't think his mother even knew before she passed."

"And you didn't think to, I don't know, warn him? Explain some of this to him?"

"It was not my place."

Now that was some royal old-fashioned bullshit. It was the way of the older mages to let their young discover their own power and then help to teach them to control it. There was a deep-seated superstition that telling a child what they *might* be would curse them against it, and they would grow up with no powers at all. Young mages stumbled around this city like bulls in a china shop, trying anything to make their powers manifest.

Like I said, old-fashioned bullshit.

"It must have killed him," I said. "Not knowing why he was the only one to survive that raid."

"You think it would have been any better if the reason was something he cannot help, a part of him that he cannot change?"

I opened my mouth to respond, but Samuel burst into the room.

"It's Peter Grassi," he said, breathless, his brown eyes shining in the overhead kitchen light. "The man on the video is Peter Grassi."

My brain launched itself into a list of possibilities.

"Get in the car."

<hr>

We sped down the interstate heading east. All the puzzle pieces snapping into place in my mind. Peter Grassi's hut on the banks of the bayou wasn't uninhabitable at all. Whoever had glamoured Grassi in the security tapes must have done something for his cabin too. If I had thought to consult with Samuel more fully throughout the investigation, I might have known that. Lucy Bettencourt might have been hidden in that glamoured shack the entire time we were looking around, and we wouldn't have had any idea.

The neighbors weren't going to be of any help. I was sure of that.

I parked my car at the end of the row of tiny ramshackle structures. I didn't want to pull to a stop in front of Grassi's place and give him time to do something dumb. The neighborhood was completely silent as we exited the car. The sounds of the bayou had even ceased, as though all anticipated that something was about to happen here. It gave me the creeps. A bullfrog would be nice right about now.

I took a step up the dirt road. The humidity of the air had tamped down the dust, so none scattered under my boots. Samuel was silent beside me, feeling the tension also. Another step, and I caught movement out of the corner of my eye. My breath hitched as a form rose from the swamp.

She was pale, her skin bloated from her death. Dark hair surrounded her like a veil and her white night gown was dripping with bayou filth. She raised a finger and pointed at me. This wasn't good. This was neither the time nor the place to have to deal with the dead. Not when I was trying to save the living.

I waved a hand and silently commanded her back to her watery grave, wishing I had taken Florentina up on her offer to teach me better shields against this kind of threat. The spirit wasn't strong enough to resist my power, and without a sound she descended again beneath the surface of the swamp. Samuel gave me a strange look, but we continued forward silently. He hadn't seen her. His powers were nothing like mine.

Even as we approached the cabin, I hadn't seen any movement from the other structures on the row. No fae peered out at us, no inhuman eyes behind dirty windows tracked our movement this time. We got closer to the dilapi- dated building, and I let my eyes unfocus as I stared at it. Dad had taught me a bit about seeing through mild glamours. I couldn't see past any sufficiently powerful spells, but something simple, I had a chance. The image before me wavered, its edges becoming shimmery even as my eyes watered from the effort. Finally, I caught sight of the truth beneath the facade.

The porch was still falling apart in some places, but it was definitely better than I had originally thought. The windows were all mostly intact and the front door was affixed to solid metal hinges, a shiny new lock in the center of the knob. The house blocked my view of the dock behind, but I knew it would be as Samuel had described: perfectly capable of mooring a fishing boat. I blinked and the image reverted, I shook my head at the ache that was beginning to form behind my eyes. Damn, I was out of practice.

A figure rising again from the water caught my attention. The previous spirit was back again, her dark hair obscuring the left side of her face, but one dark eye fixed itself on me. I watched in horror as another figure rose beside her, this one a man. Then another, a child. I felt my breath quicken. Something had alerted them to my presence. Somehow, they knew what I was, what I could possibly do for them. But I couldn't. Not now. Not as dull as my powers were from disuse.

Sounds of tires bouncing against the dirt path and the roar of an engine caused both me and Samuel to turn around. A shiny gray vehicle sped its way up the road toward us. We dove off the path and into the yard beside the hut we had been approaching. The brakes squealed as the vehicle skidded to a halt before our target structure. I watched in horror as Darryl Georgiano stepped out of the driver's side. It had taken him almost two days to find this place after we'd given him the hint that Peter Grassi owned a cabin out here. My damn big mouth had brought him here right at the same time as the two of us.

Georgiano wore a well-tailored suit and mirrored sunglasses. The look of an old timey mob boss, I thought. He looked at Samuel and me as we rose from the lawn and gave us a smirk. A partner of his, a young man I didn't recognize, exited the passenger side of the car and ran up to Darryl's side. He wore black slacks and a white button up shirt. His red hair glinted in the sunlight as he reached behind him to the small of his back and pulled out a small black pistol.

The ghosts in the bayou were particularly still as they watched this unfold. I noted with disappointment that two more had joined the audience. Manchac had long been famous for its dead, but I sure didn't appreciate five of them staring at me at once.

"Stand back, Darryl," I called. "We were here first." Well, that sounded childish, but what else could I say?

Darryl Georgiano pulled a Glock from under his suit jacket and held it lazily at his side. "If you really want to fight over it, I'm game."

I felt Samuel stiffen beside me, but I wasn't about to turn this into a gun fight. Not when there could be an innocent girl inside that cabin. I raised my hands in a gesture of surrender. Getting Lucy home alive was more important than a feud between rival agencies. Darryl gestured and his partner approached the cabin slowly. I could tell that he too saw what I had when we'd first seen the structure, as he stepped gingerly on the front step. Realizing it truly would hold his weight, the red head hurried up the last two steps to the porch.

A shotgun blast reduced the door of the cabin to splinters.

The redhead flew back down the steps to sprawl on the dirt road. Darryl moved surprisingly fast for his massive frame and took cover behind his silver car. Samuel's arm took me around the waist, and he bore me to the ground as a collection of buck shot whizzed past where our heads had been. I lay for a moment gasping as I tried to pull air into my lungs.

Then, the ghosts attacked.

Without my voice to fight them off or banish them back

to their graves, I was nearly helpless. A set of nails scratched down my left arm as chilled hands pawed at me. They were grabbing at my skin, my clothes, whatever they could get ahold of to drag me back toward the swamp. I couldn't let that happen.

More shotgun blasts rang out, but all my attention was on the spirits. I beat at faces, arms, anything I could reach. I drove them off enough to reach into my back pocket and pull out the iron knuckles I kept there. I slipped them onto my right hand and got to my knees. The knuckles gave me a better chance, but there were still five spirits and one me.

The first ghost, all black hair and dripping clothes lunged forward and I swung. The iron met her jaw, and she reeled back, an unholy scream ripping from her lungs. The rest of the spirits hesitated, their eyes filled with desperation as they looked between the knuckles on my hand and my face. Finally, a gasp filled my lungs with air.

I poured every ounce of power I could muster into my voice. "*Begone.*"

A collective shriek from the spirits before me and they staggered and vanished from the shore. I took another deep breath, giving my chest the time to expand and heal. I turned to see Samuel still hunkered low to the ground, a pistol in his right hand as he gestured to me to get down.

I hit the earth again, catching my fall with my forearms and crawled closer to him.

"What the hell was that?" he asked.

"Long story," I said, quickly. "We need to get out of here."

"Yeah, no shit," he looked back over his shoulder. There was about twenty feet between where we lay and the house behind us. "On my signal, run for the house. I'll cover you."

I nodded my assent, and he took aim at the glamoured cabin. "One, two, three, GO!"

I took off for the cover we'd agreed on, my leather boots digging into the soft dirt of the swamp shore. I threw myself around the corner of the house and pressed my back against its wooden side. My right shoulder must have hit the corner as I'd rounded it and a deep throbbing started.

I peeked around the corner in time to see Darryl take a few shots from his vantage point behind his car. A much less fancy looking car now that it was decorated with bullet holes. "Sammy, let's go!" I yelled.

Samuel sprinted to my side and gripped my shoulders, spinning us both around the wooden wall to cover. I cried out as his thumb drove into my right shoulder.

"What happened? Are you okay?" his voice was a desperation as his eyes raked me over.

I'm fine, I thought. I just banged my arm.

"Mer, you got hit!"

The hell? I looked down at my right shoulder. The warm red blood that was flowing down my arm. Damn it.

I sank down the wall as my knees gave out. Shot? I'd never been shot before. Is this what being shot felt like? I was completely numb. But I could see the bright red blood and I could feel some dull throbbing. Maybe this was what being shot was like for everyone? Samuel pulled his shirt over his head, exposing the white undershirt beneath. He pressed the fabric to the back of my shoulder, and I smothered a yell. Damn, that stung. This always looked so much cooler in the movies.

"I have to get you to a hospital," he said.

"No!" I said, quickly. I didn't have time to explain, but I couldn't let him do that. "No hospital. Take me to Brigitte."

I gave him the address quickly and made him repeat it

back twice before I was satisfied he knew it. I couldn't count on staying conscious long enough to direct him myself.

"I need to get you to the car," he said.

I nodded.

"This is going to hurt."

I gritted my teeth. He hauled me to my feet, and I saw stars. Slinging my good arm around his shoulders, he half dragged me to our car. We stayed close to the line of houses, out of sight of whoever was still firing shots at Darryl in the street.

We were just going to leave him there, I realized. He would have done the same to us, I knew, but damn, that felt cold.

Samuel shoved me in through the passenger side of the car with hurried apologies as my shoulder was jostled. A second later he jumped into the front seat. He threw the car into reverse and backed us off the dirt road. I grimaced as the unpaved street bounced our car around, sending spikes of pain through my shoulder.

I could feel my flesh trying to heal around the bullets that were embedded there. If it closed completely, at least I wouldn't bleed out, but it would really suck when Brigitte had to open it again to pull out the lead. The edges of my vision were growing fuzzy, darkening from the trauma as my body tried to heal itself.

"Whatever you do," I whispered. "No hospital."

Samuel was silent and I threw my left hand over and gripped his thigh.

"No hospital," I said, again. "Promise me."

I could see his jaw working against his objections. "No hospital," he finally agreed.

"Thank you," I whispered and let that darkness swallow me up.

# Chapter Twelve

Brigitte le Blanc was a healer. It wasn't just her profession; it was her being. If you had a bad day, she had a kind word. If you had a paper cut, she had a bandage. And if you had a half dozen tiny balls of lead embedded in your shoulder, she had a cold white examination table and bright lights that shone in your eyes.

I squinted into those lights now.

"Ow, dammit, Brigitte," I complained as her hands manipulated the skin that had healed over the buckshot on the drive over.

"Lie still and stop being such a baby," Brigitte said. Like I said, a healer.

"Careful." Samuel's voice from the corner of the room.

"Shut up," we both told him.

I sat cross legged on that cold table. Brigitte had cut down the sleeves of my t-shirt so it pooled around my waist. I was grateful we hadn't had to cut off my sports bra as well. Not that I was a prude. It was my favorite bra.

I squeezed my eyes shut as I felt Brigitte digging around under my skin before making a triumphant sound. The plink of one lead BB landing in a metal tray sounded through the room and I peeked through my lashes to see Samuel turning green.

Super.

"Brigitte," I warned. "You're about to have two patients."

"Goshdarnit," the healer said, magicking her hands clean with a shake as she crossed the room and gripped Samuel under the arm. "You, get out. Wait in the hall. Sit *down* somewhere and try not to puke on my furniture."

I chuckled to myself until Brigitte came back and smacked my shoulder.

"You're worse than the shifters."

I craned my neck to see what she meant. The skin had healed back over my shoulder in the amount of time it had taken her to throw Samuel out. Dammit. I wasn't a shifter, but yeah, my healing abilities were second to none.

"I'm going to have to keep the wound open to clear it out."

"I know."

"It's not going to feel nice."

"Do your worst."

Brigitte gave me a grim smile and her hands began to glow. I closed my eyes again as she placed her palms on my skin. It didn't start too bad. A warm feeling that traveled along my shoulder and back causing goosebumps to break out along my abdomen. Then the warmth traveled deeper into my flesh and the heat increased. I bit back an unbecoming noise as I felt the skin of my shoulder open again under her touch.

I had a long string of expletives to yell at the next shotgun I saw.

I felt a digging in my shoulder as her hands called the

lead out of my flesh and into the open air. I caught a peek at the basin beside me as the tiny orbs rained into it. One, two, three... I counted as they dropped into the container, their sound like the toll of a clock tower as they chimed against the metal base. Four more BBs joined the first that Brigitte had pulled out of me.

I sighed with relief as I felt her mending my shoulder back together. It wasn't a crude needle and thread that she used. Her hands called to the muscle, binding it closed the way only a magical healer could. I could sense her fatigue as she finished, the skin sealing beneath her hands.

"Okay," she said finally, shaking the glow from her hands. "You're done."

My shoulder was tight. My right arm not quite ready to throw a ball, but at least it was clear of foreign objects now.

"Just don't strain it," Brigitte said. She picked up the basin and walked it to the sink across the room from me. "I'm tired of you re-injuring my work."

I was ready to protest, but she was right. I couldn't think of a single time when she had healed me that I hadn't turned around and undone her work by participating in something stupid. Normally there was a good reason for it, but that excuse wouldn't fly in this room.

"Go get yourself cleaned up," Brigitte said. "You can use the bath through my bedroom."

I thanked her and hopped off the table. Brigitte's home was as familiar to me as my own. Many a night I had stayed here when we were studying our way through university classes that seemed to never end. She had a spare bedroom that we'd almost started calling mine before Dad had found the house I owned now.

I walked through her pristine bedroom. The bed was made, a dozen or so throw pillows that were *not for sleeping* covered most of the bedspread. Unlike my room, there were no clothes dropped on the floor which could certainly be worn another time but weren't quite clean enough to hang up in the closet with the truly fresh clothes. The figurines on top of her dresser were organized into tiny armies. I'd bought her most of those, ceramic fairies and dragons that caught her eye but that she wouldn't buy for herself.

I caught a glimpse of myself in the mirror over the dresser and did a double take. Dirt caked my face and forearms from when I'd been dragged across the ground. The claws that had grabbed at my arm had left reddened streaks behind, but they had healed closed, probably long before we made it back to the city proper. My right arm was covered in congealed blood, it looked like too much for one person to survive losing, but my body replaced blood quickly. I was lucky. If I was fully human, we may not have made it to Brigitte's before I lost too much.

I turned the shower on in the bathroom and stripped my bra off awkwardly, trying not to contort my right shoulder too badly in doing so. I kicked my muddy boots to the corner of the bathroom and shimmied out of my pants and the remnants of my butchered t-shirt.

The heat from the shower was amazing, purifying. I stepped under the waterfall showerhead and let it wash the day away. The caddy that Brigitte had affixed to the wall held a variety of different scented body washes and shampoos. I nearly broke the hairband as I dragged it out of my hair and shook my brown locks out under the stream of water.

The first bottle my hand touched contained a combination of spearmint and eucalyptus. It proudly proclaimed *Stress Relief* on the front. I figured I could use some of that.

I would have liked to fill the tub and soak in it, but we didn't have time for me to luxuriate.

We still didn't know if Lucy was even *in* that Manchac cabin. If Darryl hadn't shown up and interrupted our advance on the house, would we have found the answers we sought, or would we have been no better than his redheaded partner, bleeding out in the street. I shook away the image of Samuel being the one lying there, his life seeping into the dirt.

I turned off the shower and toweled dry. In Brigitte's room, I dug through the drawers of the dresser, being careful not to litter the floor with them. Brigitte and I were close to the same size. I pulled on a pair of her jeans and a t-shirt with the logo of a cafe we'd both frequented far too often in college.

I found Samuel and Brigitte back in the living room. For how dark his Cajun heritage normally made his skin, Samuel somehow managed to look pale from his ordeal watching Brigitte heal me. Or maybe it was the package of fetal pigs that Brigitte was again sorting through. I smirked. It wouldn't surprise me if she pulled them out specially to show him.

"You want some coffee or something?" I asked, walking past them and into the kitchen.

Samuel seemed to want to look anywhere except at Brigitte. "I'll help," he said quickly and followed me.

He leaned against the counter as I pulled out the coffee maker and searched the cupboards for filters.

"So," he began. "Your best friend is a mage."

"Your grandma is a fortune teller," I pointed out.

"Sure," he said. He pulled a box of coffee filters from the counter behind him and passed them to me. "But that's not real magic. She just has gullible clients."

I didn't argue with him. It wouldn't do any good.

"Most humans can't use magic," Samuel said. "It's unnatural."

I crossed my arms. "I won't let you insult Brigitte, especially not in her own home. Magic abandoned the humans because they abused it. Those whose families treated the magic well still have mages born to them. It's not Brigitte's fault she was born a mage. She's chosen to use that power to help people, to heal people. There's nothing more natural, more human than using what you can to help your fellow man."

"It's not a trick then? The magic is real. She's not just waving her hand and saying, 'hocus pocus diagnosus' and making something up?"

I nearly laughed. "You saw how she fixed my shoulder. Did that look like a trick to you?"

"Are you saying that not all of Grand-mère's clients are simply gullible?"

"There are more *normal* humans in this city who practice magic than most people want to believe," I said. "It's easier to organize people into groups and say, this whole swath of the population is dangerous and the rest of us are okay, but that's hardly ever true. Peter Grassi is no mage and look what he's done."

Samuel seemed to ponder that a moment. "What made you want to go back to that cabin?"

I filled the coffee filter with more grounds than was probably advisable, but I needed the strong stuff.

"You asked me what I'd seen when we first visited," he continued. "And when I told you, you wanted to go back. You hadn't believed anything was there before then."

I pushed the start button on the coffee maker and turned to face him. "Okay, you got me, officer."

He scowled.

"Too soon?"

"A little, yeah."

"Sorry," I grabbed three mugs out of the cupboard and set them on the countertop. I took a breath to steel myself. I had to tell him. I owed it to him to tell him the truth about what he was. Maybe he was ready.

"Have you ever heard of a Nullifier?"

Samuel shook his head.

"There are plenty of different kinds of magic. There's magic that's trained for combat, healing, historical preservation. There are magical artifacts and magical creatures," I paused a moment, trying to find the best way to explain it. "A Nullifier is an anti-magical being."

"Anti-magic," Samuel said.

"Like a magical black hole," I said. "A mage can cast spells to damage and a Nullifier will feel none of them. The spell will pass right through them and leave them unharmed. It's an extremely rare ability. Most people go their whole lives without ever meeting a Nullifier. I mean, the power isn't foolproof. A mage can use a spell to heft a rock at a Nullifier and the physical rock may still find its mark, but a direct spell attack?" I shook my head.

"And you think whoever took Lucy was a Nullifier?"

I pushed my damp hair back from my forehead. "No, that's not what I'm saying." I drew in a deep breath, the smell of coffee tickling the back of my nose. "When we first visited Peter Grassi's cabin, I didn't see what you saw."

"What does that mean?"

"I mean, I saw an uninhabitable building that was inches from falling down. A structure that wouldn't hold even my weight. A dock that was half submerged in the swamp, entirely unusable."

Samuel raised an eyebrow.

"It was glamoured, Sammy," I said slowly. "I can't see through glamour without intense concentration, but a Nullifier..." I trailed off, hoping he'd understand.

Samuel's hand shook and he gripped the counter beside him.

"And on the surveillance footage from the Bettencourts," he said, slowly.

"I never saw a thing. A slight shimmering maybe where you pointed out the figure to me, but I never saw a man in that video."

"You're telling me that I'm—" he choked on the word and tried again. "That I'm a Nullifier?"

"It's the only explanation," I said.

I could see the turmoil on his face, his brows drew low over his eyes as he considered my words

I dropped my voice to a whisper. "No one survives Mage's Fire, Sammy. No one."

That sent him over the edge. "I have to go."

Before I could say anything, he had left the kitchen. He moved quickly, through the living room and out the front door. His steps were like hammers thudding on the front steps, pounding in my chest.

I walked past a stunned Brigitte and heard the car start. Damn it, he had my keys. A voice in the back of my head told me to let him go. I hoped he'd come back. I hoped he wouldn't do something stupid before he did.

I turned back to Brigitte's questioning eyes.

"Coffee?" I asked, giving her an I-don't-want-to-talk-about-it smile.

"Are those my clothes?"

"No?" I walked back into the kitchen.

"Yes, to the coffee!" she called from the living room.

I returned to the living room with two steaming mugs and handed one to the healer.

"Thanks," I said. "For the shoulder."

I could see the weariness in her face from the effort it had taken to heal me.

"It's nothing," she said. She raised her mug in a toasting motion and took a sip. "Eugh, Meranda you are *never* making coffee again."

I pulled my legs up onto the couch to avoid getting stepped on as she made her way to the kitchen in search of cream.

"Sorry," I called. "I like it strong."

"You're an animal."

I picked a book off the coffee table and pulled it into my lap. The illustrated biology. Awesome. I flipped through the pages and tried to ignore the weight of the cell phone in my pocket. I wanted Samuel to call. I wanted him to turn around and come back to talk about it. But I remembered back to when I'd first learned what I was. The powers I wielded. I'd run away too.

"A Punnett Square," Brigitte said, coming back into the room.

"A what?"

She nodded at the book in my hands, the colorful diagram on the page. "That's a Punnett Square."

She sat on the couch beside me and tapped a finger on the page. "We use them to determine inherited genotypes from the known parent's genotype."

"Ah," I said.

"Last year we used them to determine blood type in class. It was kind of a disaster."

"The four-by-four grid was a disaster?"

Brigitte took a sip from her, now nearly white, coffee

and grimaced. "We took the ABO blood type of each student's parent and created the square so we could find the possible combinations that would result in that students blood type."

I looked at her sideways.

"What? It's a completely normal experiment to run in high school biology!"

I was grateful she was distracting me, so I nodded and let her continue.

"Anyway, we found out that one kid's parents weren't actually her parents."

"What?"

"Well, her dad anyway," she said. "Pretty sure her mom remembered birthing her."

"Did the dad know?"

"I'm not sure," Brigitte said. "The mom told the kid that there must have been some mistake with the experiment because of course she was their child." Brigitte shrugged. "The science doesn't lie."

I could imagine the horror that mother had felt. The horror the *kid* must have felt.

"Thanks," I said. "For trying to distract me."

She nodded and we both sipped our coffees in silence for a moment. I flipped past a few of the more graphic images in the illustrated book.

"He'll come back," she said. I wasn't sure how much she'd heard from our conversation in the kitchen. "I saw the concern he had for you. He'll come back."

I reached a hand out and squeezed her arm. "Thanks."

My phone rang, startling us both.

"Hello?"

"Miss Meranda?"

"Freyja, what's going on?"

"It's Lucy," she said. "Please come now."

At the desperation in her voice my heart sank to somewhere beneath my feet. "I'm on my way."

---

The driveway in front of the Bettencourt house was filled with more NOPD squad cars than I'd seen in my life. A white van with the words CORONER painted on the side had pulled up the gravel almost directly to the grassy lawn. Once manicured in straight mown lines, dozens of pairs of trampling feet had reduced the green to a muddy mess as the facade of perfection was turned over to ugliness. I couldn't see much through those rows of tightly packed legs as I jogged up the driveway from the street, but I did catch a glimpse of a pair of small legs, tennis shoe missing from one foot, a pink sock exposed. Then the dark waterproof bag was zipped up and I couldn't see anymore. *Oh, Lucy.*

I didn't have much time to react to what I'd seen before Freyja was before me, pawing at the front of my shirt, pushing me back down the drive. "I shouldn't have called you," she said hurriedly. "I'm sorry. I really shouldn't have called you."

"What do you mean?" I grabbed her hands so she would stop pushing at me and held her still. "You were right to call me. Now tell me honestly, was that Lucy?"

Freyja's impossibly large eyes filled with tears and her lower lip trembled. She nodded once and squeezed her eyes shut. My heart had taken up permanent residence in the soles of my boots and it ached at the confirmation.

"YOU!" The snarl pulled my attention away from the fae before me.

"YOU DID THIS!"

Mrs. Bettencourt descended on the pair of us like a vengeful harpy, all dark clothes and perfect makeup. Her heels wouldn't dare stick into the gravel of the driveway despite the force of her strides toward us. I pushed Freyja behind me just in time to receive an open-handed slap from Louisa Bettencourt's right arm.

She hit like a woman raised in luxury, but still it stung. I pressed my left hand to my cheek and held up my right, trying to put distance between myself and the flailing arms before me.

"You did this," Louisa wailed. "If we hadn't consulted with your *incompetent* organization my Lucy would still be ali-i-ive." The last word turned to a sob. I caught the woman as she crumpled to the gravel.

I held Louisa Bettencourt as her sobs shook us both and the truth of what she'd said hammered into my chest.

Mr. Bettencourt caught up to us then, his face paler than I'd ever seen it. All blood had drained from his lips and cheeks, leaving dark bags under his eyes and red rimming their glossy surface.

"I will thank you to take your hands off of my wife, Miss Haley," he spat my name out like it was poison on his lips. A half dozen officers had broken away from the group on the lawn and were advancing on our strange meeting.

I pushed away from Mrs. Bettencourt and stood as Richard Bettencourt raised his wife to her feet. He tucked her protectively under his arm where she sagged into his side, all strength seemingly gone.

"Mr. Georgiano told us the whole story," Mr. Bettencourt said. "He told us how you botched the whole investigation and tipped off our daughter's kidnappers and now she's—she's—"

Mrs. Bettencourt wailed again.

I wanted to shake my head. I wanted to deny it, to tell them that the Georgianos had gone toward that cabin guns blazing when a more subtle approach would have served well. But I couldn't deny that it was my fault. I had let slip that Peter Grassi had another address. I had been the one to set the Georgianos on that line of inquiry. It was my fault that they were there that day. If I hadn't said anything in front of them, Lucy might still be alive.

Mrs. Bettencourt seemed to return to herself with one last burst of strength, she stood up straight beside her husband and pointed a finger at my chest. "You, get off our property. If we ever see you here again, we will prosecute."

I put both hands up and took a step backward.

"Freda," Mr. Bettencourt snapped his fingers. "Come back to the house. I believe Mrs. Bettencourt needs to lie down."

I looked at the fae beside me. Something akin to fear lit in the back of her wide eyes. I saw her throat working. I thought she would leave. That she would rid herself of these employers who hadn't taken the time to learn her name or appreciate what she could do for them. I'd seen fae employed to their full potential when their magic was cultivated, not feared. She could do well elsewhere.

"Now." Mr. Bettencourt snapped his fingers again and Freyja jumped. Her eyes immediately fixed on the gravel below her feet, and she stepped across the space to Mrs. Bettencourt. She took the woman's arm and led her back to the house.

"My wife is far more forgiving than I am, Miss Haley," Mr. Bettencourt hissed. "If I see you anywhere near our home again, I will kill you myself."

The officers who had walked toward us had stopped a respectful distance away, but I knew they could hear the threat he made. I knew, also, that they would ignore such a thing. That every officer there would swear under oath if my body ever turned up somewhere that Mr. Bettencourt *hadn't* said such things and that he couldn't possibly have anything to do with it.

This was no place to confront him for his words or the wicked gleam I saw in his eye at the prospect of killing me. I'd known grieving families. I'd seen the way humans respond to grief in unique ways in every situation. The way it amplified emotions to an untenable level until they spilled over in completely uncharacteristic outbursts. I inclined my head to Richard Bettencourt and backed a few paces down the drive before turning to walk away.

With each step my chest ached more and more. A child was dead. She was dead because of me. Nothing I did now could change that. It didn't matter that the Bettencourts had kicked me off the case. It didn't matter that I would never be paid for the investigating that I had done. Their little girl was dead because of me.

I should never have taken the case.

I wandered the city for nearly an hour. My steps were heavy, my boots felt water-logged, but still I walked. Part of me wanted to go to Baxter's to touch that dog's silky ears and have Charlie joke with me and make me feel better. A stronger part of me knew that if I sat at that bar, I would drink. I would drink hard liquor that stung on the way down and softened the edges of the world just enough that I wouldn't feel their sharpness digging into my heart. But I couldn't do that. I couldn't keep a leash on my powers if I did that. Not that I was entirely invisible to the spirits as it was. The static clung to me.

Banishing those five spirits on the banks of the Manchac bayou had left a beacon on my head again. I knew it wasn't quite bright enough for the spirits of the city to pinpoint me, but they were drawn near me. Their forms blinked in and out of sight as they jostled along with the other pedestrians on the sidewalk. I was sure they didn't fully know why they were drawn to this particular part of the city. They didn't know who I was or what I could do for them, they just knew they were magnetized toward me. A strange ghostly parade that flanked me as I made my way around the city and closer to my neighborhood.

I could feel the weight of those souls, dragging on my limbs like an anchor. Their horror and fear in their last moments as potent to me as any strong drink. I absorbed it gratefully, replacing the stabbing guilt with the agony of those damned to wander these streets. It wasn't a pleasant exchange and it left me gasping, but it was just different enough that I didn't feel as though I was drowning anymore.

I made it to my neighborhood, and Joseph seemed to sense that I didn't want to talk. He wordlessly unlocked the gate for me and held it as I passed through. The spirits trailed me up the street of the quiet neighborhood. The well-kept lawns reminded me of the Bettencourt's before it had been trampled under the feet of NOPD's finest. Before the dead body of their daughter had been thrown upon it.

The clamoring of ghostly voices increased in volume and urgency as my followers began to realize that I was the only one on the street and I *must* be the source of the draw they felt. Spirit hands drifted toward becoming corporeal as they reached for me, tearing at my clothes as I advanced up the walkway toward my front door. I couldn't blame them for the desperation they felt. So close to one whom they thought could give them release, could finally give them rest. But I could not. Despite all the power that lay in my core, I had never learned to bring relief to the spirits that my powers drew to me. It was a limbo, a purgatory that I offered them, to be so close to me, yet never find what they sought.

A last clawed hand on my right shoulder tore the sleeve from my arm as I finally reached the green painted door. A key in the lock, a twist of the knob, and I was inside. The warding that Florentina had placed on the house held firm. The voices on my lawn gave a distressed cry as the light they had been drawn to blinked out of their sight leaving them cold and empty, purposeless. I hated how much I related to that.

I pressed my back against the wooden door. My knees gave out then, and I sank down, nearly banging the back of my head against the wood frame. The entryway rug bunched in the middle as my heels pushed it across the hardwood. A cool breeze drifted across the floor and caressed my cheeks where I sat as the one ghost I would never want to cast away, even if I knew how, settled herself beside me.

Marie Breton's touch was cool against my exposed shoulder. A hand of comfort that I didn't deserve. I drew my knees up to my chest and rested my forehead against them.

"I screwed up," I said.

I soft shushing sound beside me, like a mother with a small child. That was enough to send me over the edge and I wept into my knees.

Marie's presence left my side a few moments later and I heard the landline knocked off its cradle. Someone had been calling, I realized. I had thought the ringing was in my ears, a whine that traveled up from my trampled heart, but no. Someone had been trying to get ahold of me. I curled on my side beside the entry way table wishing for nothing more than the floor to swallow me up, take me away from this place.

I could hear the muffled sound of Florentina's voice through the phone receiver calling my name into the empty living room. I put my arms over my head. An ominous wailing sound from Marie, the desperate cry of a spirit who is not yet strong enough to form words and Florentina hung up.

A jacket was knocked off the hooks on the wall, Marie's doing, no doubt. It floated down too perfectly to cover my back and shoulders, to warm my chilled frame. I closed my eyes, willing myself away, to anywhere else.

A knock on my front door and a key turning in the lock. Only one person had a key to this place other than me.

"Dad?" I asked.

"Afraid not, girl," Florentina walked into the entryway, her skirts swishing against the floorboards.

I closed my eyes again. "Leave me alone."

"Don't be so damn dramatic," my aunt said. "It's unbecoming. Bring her to the living room."

I let out a squawk of surprise that truly was unbecoming as strong arms wrapped behind my knees and shoulders and I was hefted close to a firm chest. I breathed in the scent of Samuel's cologne and buried my face into his shoulder.

"Hey, Mer," he whispered. "Hang on, grandma will take care of you."

I let out a weak protest as he set me on the couch in the living room and his warmth left me.

"You are a silly, foolish girl," Florentina said. She ran her hands over my shoulders. My skin warmed beneath her touch. "How many of them did you allow to touch you?"

"Just now or at Manchac?" I asked, my teeth began to chatter as the jacket that had covered me was removed.

"Foolish girl," Florentina repeated.

I gasped as she pressed a palm to my chest pushing what felt like a shard of ice into my sternum.

"You should have been shielded. You should have known how to defend against this," Florentina chastised as I took in another sharp breath.

I realized then that the weight that crushed my chest wasn't only due to the words Mrs. Bettencourt had said or the enormity of how badly I'd cost their family. It was the touch of the dead.

"H-how did you know?" I asked, my breath fogged the air in front of my face. Shit, this was bad.

"We saw on the news that Lucy's body was found," Samuel said. "We couldn't get ahold of your cell phone, so we called here."

I nodded and tried to hold my teeth together to still their chatter. If Marie hadn't answered the call, they may not have come in time.

"Samuel, go find some extra blankets," Florentina ordered. "And Marie, dear, please step back. I know you want to help, but you will not warm her."

A distressed noise sounded from the corner of the room and then I heard noises from the upstairs where Marie spent most of her time. I'd apologize to her later. It wasn't her fault I'd ended up this way. Samuel returned with piles of old quilts and blankets from the hall closet and soon I was nearly smothered under them.

"I'll put some tea on," Florentina said, rising from my side. "I've done all I can do for now. Your body must do the rest."

I nodded and closed my eyes, feeling my chest thaw ever so slowly. Each ice crystal beneath my skin melted with a small stabbing sensation, but the largest pieces had been broken up by Florentina's ministrations, and what was left felt more like brushing against sandpaper than a knife to the chest.

The couch shifted as Samuel sat beside me. His warm hand on my forehead pushed the hair back from my face.

"What did this?" he asked.

My first impulse was to hide from him, to shrink back. I'd spent my entire life hiding who I was, what I could do. It was habit to lie about it all. But I knew about him. I'd shattered his whole world with what I'd told him earlier that day. I could trust him with this. Surely, I owed him that much.

"We live in one of the most haunted cities in the world," I said. I took his hand between my own and turned it over in my hands, examining the back of it. Slightly raised scars whose stories I didn't know stood out pale against his dark skin. "You've heard of ghost sickness?"

"Normal people don't get ghost sickness," Samuel said. His words an assurance to himself that what I was saying couldn't be true.

"No," I said. "But untrained Potesta Spirituum do."

Samuel drew his hand back. I'd expected such a reaction, but it still tugged at my heart that he'd drawn away so fast.

"Potesta," he whispered. *Power, Authority.* What I was. The title my kind had been given.

"Untrained?" he asked. His disapproval was the same as his grandmother's. I tried to shrug. The mound of blankets twitched at my effort.

"Tante tried," I said. "I was taken away in the middle of her lessons for more pressing matters. By the time I came back to the city, I was too old for the training to be natural. And I was a stubborn teenager who didn't want to work for it."

"Ah,"

"Yeah," I said. "I know enough to banish the spirits, to control some of their actions, but not enough to help them cross over. To give them peace."

"And they are attracted to you," he said.

"Moreso when I've already interacted with one," I said. "It leaves a mark of some kind. Like a neon sign saying, 'here's someone who can help you, come talk to her', but I can't. Tante can cleanse that away, but I didn't see her after Manchac."

"When all hell broke loose," Samuel said. "And you were staring out into the bayou. There were ghosts then."

I nodded.

"And what attracted them to you?" he asked. "Had you seen more that day?"

"It's complicated," I whispered.

Florentina saved me from having to explain. She walked back into the room carrying a tea service that I had buried back in a China hutch and forgotten about. Samuel helped me sit up, arranging the blankets around my shoulders so I could take the porcelain cup that Florentina handed me.

"You could have died," Florentina said as she sat in an armchair across from me.

"I know, Tante," I said. I stared down into the cup, breathing in the steam that curled up from its depths.

"What were you thinking, walking through these streets undefended, unshielded?"

"I wasn't thinking," I said. I thought about all the times I could have stopped; could have run to the Agency and shaken the ghosts off. And the weight of despair that had settled upon me after seeing Lucy's body, the way I just hadn't cared about the spirits that could have killed me. "I don't know."

"Foolish girl," Florentina said.

"Cheers," I raised my glass and took a sip.

"What now?" Samuel asked, leaning back beside me on the couch.

"The Bettencourts fired us," I said.

"Really?"

I shrugged again. "I don't blame them."

"Hey," Samuel said. "What happened was not our fault. Darryl Georgiano would have tipped them off whether we had been there or not."

"Darryl Georgiano wouldn't have known that cabin even existed if it hadn't been for me," I said. "It doesn't matter. The Bettencourts hired us for a kidnapping, to bring their daughter home *safely*. Can't do that now."

"I hate this," Samuel said.

"Me too."

The tea was doing its job. I was beginning to feel like myself again, and I dropped a few blankets off my shoulders.

"So, what now?" Samuel asked.

"Maybe there's work at the Academy this week. Maybe I can bring in enough to pay off some of the Agency's debts," I said.

"I can work some small cases," Samuel said. "If you let me, I mean."

"Of course," I said. "You have a real talent for this."

Florentina dropped a hand onto the end table beside her chair with enough force to make me jump. "I cannot believe the two of you," she said. "You act as if this is over. As though it is done."

"The Bettencourts fired us," I said. "I don't know what you'd want me to do."

"You talk to that girl," Florentina said. "If it really is your fault that she was killed, if you really are responsible, you owe it to that child to bring her some peace. Murdered children do not get peace automatically, Potesta."

I flinched at the title.

"It is your job to give that to her."

"How do you expect me to do that?" I asked. "I have no idea where to even begin."

Florentina made a scoffing noise.

"We bring her killers to justice," Samuel said quietly beside me.

I tried not to gawk at him.

"It makes sense," he said. "Ghosts linger when they have unfinished business, when they have secrets that are hurting them. That's why deathbed confessions are so common, people instinctively know that that is their only path to rest."

"Exactly," Florentina said. "So, you will finish this case, you will find the killer, and you will give that child some peace."

I couldn't believe what I was hearing. I couldn't believe that most of it made sense. One problem though: I still didn't know how to help Lucy Bettencourt pass on.

"Where do we start?" I asked.

"You could talk to your father again," Florentina said. "He knows more about your abilities than anyone."

I clenched my jaw. It seemed to me that talking to my father is what helped get me into this mess in the first place. But I couldn't deny that Florentina was right. My father had a hand in creating what I was. He might be able to help.

"I'll try to get some more information on who dumped the body," Samuel said. "If Peter Grassi was behind all of this, he certainly didn't work alone."

An image flashed unbidden into my mind of Mr. Bettencourt's threats of the glint behind his eyes that told me he was perfectly capable of murder.

"Look into the Bettencourts more," I said. "Richard especially. There's a reason he lied about seeing Grassi recently, I want to know what it is."

I threw the rest of the blankets off and stood up. "Did you bring the car?"

"It's outside," Florentina said, a half-smile curving her mouth. "Where do you want to go?"

"Back to the Agency, we've got calls to make," I said.

"And I want to talk to my father."

# Chapter Thirteen

"Dad?"

"Hey, kiddo."

I sank deeper into the cushions of the couch, easing at the familiar sound of his voice. I had explored more of his apartment this visit. A glass that I'd grown up drinking from, sat on the coffee table before me, filled with water from the sink. It wasn't so strange to be here anymore, almost relaxing. Like before I'd left, the safety I'd been looking for was here in this room.

"We lost the kid."

A sigh. A heavy, deep sigh. The kind that only someone who understands your pain can give you.

"I'm sorry," he said. I knew he meant it.

"Yeah." I took a deep breath. "I need to talk to her. I need to find out what happened."

"Is that why you called me up, Meranda?"

"I don't know how to turn it off," I said. "Once I talk to a spirit, I don't know how to fend off the others."

"You need to focus."

I could have groaned. The number of times I'd heard that exact phrase growing up, from Florentina, from him...

"How?" I asked. "Give me the steps."

"It's not that simple."

"How can it not be that simple?" My voice came out higher pitched than I wanted, but there it was. Desperation. "There has to be some kind of formula. Or at least instructions of some kind!"

A sigh again, a frustrated one. Another sound with which I was supremely well-acquainted. The light above my head flickered and I glared at it. I'd have to change that bulb. Someone should be here, taking care of this place. He should be here.

"What do you feel when you are speaking to a spirit? When one of them is speaking to you?" His tone was patient, beyond what I deserved.

I closed my eyes and thought about it. I tried to remember what I'd felt when Sarah had talked to me, when the ghosts on the streets had torn at my skin. "Scared," I said finally.

"You feel that because you are not in control," my father said. "You conquer that fear, you control that fear, you control the situation. Then, you can command them."

He made it sound so simple. As though fear was something you could turn off and on like a light switch.

"Conquer the fear?" I asked. "Any tricks for that?"

A chuckle, low and deep. It seemed to envelope me, embrace me.

"I wish you were here," I whispered.

"Me too, kiddo."

The silence stretched. A lump rose in my throat, threatening to choke me.

"I wish you hadn't died," I said into the empty room.

A long pause. "Me too, kiddo."

---

I was halfway down the stairs when my phone rang. Unknown number. I picked it up.

"Meranda Haley," I said.

"Meranda," a deep voice greeted me. "It's Geoff Harnock. I just saw the news."

I rubbed a hand down my face pushing down the flooding emotions.

"Yeah," I said finally. What else was I supposed to say?

"Artemus told me that she was the one who posted the ransom in the school," he said. His voice like sandpaper. "If that had anything to do with it. If she distracted you so that you didn't reach that little girl in time—"

"She didn't," I told him. "Whatever we could have done differently to get to Lucy, it certainly wasn't Artemus' fault."

A grunt sounded from the other end of the line. Unconvinced. "Either way, she will be disciplined. I failed to keep her in line."

A lump rose in my throat again. "Don't," I said. "Don't punish her. Don't take away her cell phone or wake her up at five in the morning for a training session."

"What?"

"Why do you think she did it, Geoff?"

"I told you already, because I didn't keep her in line."

I could have banged my head against the stair wall beside me. "No," I said. "She wants you. She wants to get your attention and the only way she thinks she can is by acting out. This wasn't disrespect; it was desperation."

A pause sounded. "And if I give in, isn't that rewarding her for her behavior."

I stepped down the last step and started up the narrow hallway. "Just try it out," I said. "Don't take her to a training session, take her to get ice cream. Ask her about her day. Ask her about her friends. She doesn't need a commanding officer, Geoff. She needs a dad."

When he spoke again, the gruffness was back. "I'll think about it. And Meranda, you should join us for training sometime. Someone as small as you, doing the work you do? You'd be knocked right off your feet if someone had a half a mind to do so."

"Thanks for the vote of confidence," I said.

"It's not an insult," Geoff said, his voice softening. "It's just a fact."

"I'll keep it in mind," I said. "Go hug your daughter."

I hung up the phone.

---

Samuel looked up from the computer as I walked into my dad's office.

"Any answers from your dad?"

I leaned against the desk and pulled open the top left drawer. "Control my fear, control the ghosts?"

"That easy huh?" Samuel asked. "You want me to help you practice? I can jump out and scare you when you come around corners and stuff."

"Sure, that'll solve it." I pulled a packet of pretzels from the drawer and broke it open. Damn, I was starving. Nearly dying will do that to you, I supposed.

"I don't know if it'll help," Samuel said. "But I've always

found courage to be more of a fake it 'til you make it situation."

"Yeah?" I asked. "You think the ghosts will be fooled by a brave face."

"It's possible," Samuel said. "Most people are."

I craned my neck to see the computer screen. "Did you find anything interesting?"

"Quite a bit actually," Samuel said, turning the monitor so I could get a better view. "Did you know Mr. Bettencourt isn't actually rich?"

"Don't be ridiculous," I said. "You've seen their house. They're loaded."

Samuel shook his head. "*Mrs.* Bettencourt is loaded. All the businesses are in her name. I think they came from her father. Richard Bettencourt married into it."

Something in the back of my mind told me that this was incredibly important. Something about motive. "Pre-nup?"

"Bulletproof," Samuel said. "If she leaves, she takes everything with her."

I sat back on the dark wood of the desk. Huh. Something about that smelled of motive, but Louisa Bettencourt wasn't the one who died. Why would Richard kill their daughter?

Unless...

"Was there ever a paternity test run on Lucy?"

Samuel gave me a strange look. "Not from what I know. What are you thinking?"

"Just something that Brigitte said. I think I need to make a call."

"Wait a minute," Samuel said. "There's one more thing."

He made a few clicks on the computer and a new screen

popped up. The headlines of The Crescent City Enquirer. "A gossip column, really?"

"Just look," Samuel said.

I looked. Holy shit.

"Mrs. Bettencourt was committed?"

Samuel nodded. "They're saying the grief of losing their daughter made her snap. She was taken to a mental institution literally *hours* after Lucy was discovered."

"Let me guess," I said. "Richard Bettencourt is her medical power of attorney. He's the one who got her committed?"

"Ding, ding, ding," Samuel said. "That still doesn't explain how he was able to glamour the cabin or Grassi for the flash drive drop off."

"Yeah," I said. "I don't imagine Peter Grassi has that kind of power just lying around."

But... Richard Bettencourt did. He had access to a fae. In his own house.

"I'll be right back," I said quickly. "Don't go anywhere."

---

Freyja picked up on the second ring, a habit I could get used to. It was nice to have something you could rely on in this uncertain world, even if it was just the phone etiquette of others.

"Freyja, it's Meranda Haley."

A pause. A shuffling noise as though the phone had been shifted. My mind conjured images of the housekeeper looking around furtively to make sure no one was listening in. Maybe she hid around a corner like a character in an overly dramatic stage production.

"You shouldn't be calling here," she said finally, a bit breathless. "The Bettencourts don't want to speak to you."

"Ah, but Freyja, I'm not calling them. I'm calling you."

"Why?" Her response was short, biting. Suspicious.

"I know you helped him."

The silence stretched so long I was almost sure the line had given out. But fae could be silent. I held my breath and waited.

A stifled sob sounded, muffled by what must have been a palm pressed into the receiver of the phone.

"I know you didn't mean for her to die."

"You have to believe I didn't have a choice," Freyja whispered. "I loved Lucy. I never wanted to help him."

"I know," I said even though this was the first time I was hearing this information, because I'm *good at my job*. Take that, Sammy.

"I never wanted any of this to happen," Freyja said.

"I'm not a cop," I said. "I have no desire to prosecute anyone. I just want to know what happened. For Lucy. Doesn't she deserve that?"

A pause.

"Meet me," I said. I'd never tried to use my powers over the phone before. I wasn't even sure if Freyja needed any further prompting, but I tried. I poured some degree of command into my instructions.

"Now, or when you're off," I continued. "There's a cafe off St. Charles Avenue, right near you. La Petite Pomme de Terre."

"I'll be there," Freyja said. "Half hour."

She hung up the phone.

I had to admit, Samuel looked awfully comfortable in a small French cafe. His perfectly pressed button up and slacks, the way he crossed his legs primly, the pinky finger that he held up when he sipped his latte. I felt clunky sitting beside him.

I had been able to find a t-shirt in my old bedroom in Dad's apartment, but it sported a ridiculously aggressive logo from a band that had broken up when I was still in high school. That combined with the blue jeans I had stolen from Brigitte, tucked into my combat boots, we looked as though we had walked off set from two very different movies.

I finished the ham and cheese croissant I had ordered and sipped from the tall glass of iced coffee. I hadn't realized how hungry I was until I had walked into the small cafe and seen the selection of baked goods behind the glass of the counter. We had collected our drinks and settled at a table with a clear view of the front door. A leafy plant marched up the wall beside me and I shifted so I wouldn't brush against it. I liked this tiny cafe with its tiny croissants. I wouldn't let plant murder be on my record to keep me away from here.

Freyja walked in through the French doors. They were painted blue, and the reflection of the setting sun off of them made it appear for a moment as though the fae was under water. She looked around the room with nothing short of guilt twisting her features. She wanted to make sure no one here knew her, I realized. She didn't want anyone to know that she had met with us. I wasn't offended. In her position I'd do the same. Satisfied, she wasn't noticed, Freyja crossed the room and sat at our table.

Tucked as we were near the back of the restaurant, I was sure no one could hear us, but Freyja whispered, nonetheless. "I thought you'd be alone," she said, her eyes roamed over Samuel as though he was a predatory reptile which might strike at any moment.

"You remember Samuel," I said.

"Thanks for agreeing to meet with us," Samuel said. He leaned back in his wicker chair, the picture of relaxation. The picture of a nonthreat, I realized. He could sense her tension also.

"I shouldn't have come," Freyja said. She made as if to rise from the table, but I snaked a hand out and grasped her wrist. I poured as much compulsion into my voice as I could muster. The physical connection to her helped.

"Sit down," I said. "Relax. There's a reason you came here to begin with. You want to help Lucy. We all want to help Lucy. We want to give her peace."

Freyja seemed to deflate back into the chair. She took her arm back and clasped her hands in her lap, staring down at them instead of meeting our gaze. The guilt I could feel coming off her like waves on an ocean. It could have been overwhelming if I'd let it.

"Tell me what happened," I said. "How did Mr. Bettencourt ask you to participate?"

Freyja took in a shuddering breath and spoke. "It was a few months ago. I'd known that he had met with that uncle of theirs over the summer, but he brought him by the house also. He asked me to help glamour him against tech security. It is a simple thing. Any fae could have done it. Fooling human technology is no feat."

That's a comforting thought. How many humans felt so secure behind their walls of cameras and sensors in this city? I almost shook my head at it.

"I think it was a test," Freyja continued. "I think he

wanted to know if he *could* ask me to do things for him. Like, other things than my normal duties."

"You helped him?" I asked.

"Not at first," Freyja said. She snapped her eyes up to meet mine. A fierceness lay there. A defensiveness about her own integrity, I realized. "He threatened me. He told me that he could make it so I couldn't work for any other family in the city. That he would ruin my ability to get any job at all."

Damn, that sounded familiar.

"I'd have been destitute. I'd have to work the streets or join a family of some kind," Freyja said. "You have to believe I didn't want to do it. I didn't have a choice."

"I believe you," I said. And I did. Wasn't that exactly what Dean Chastain had told me when he wanted me to take this case. It seemed the powerful people of this city had a common threat that they chose to employ.

"I glamoured Peter Grassi," Freyja said. "Mr. Bettencourt said it had to last for a few months, but that was no trouble. The glamour lasts until I strip it away."

"Isn't that draining?" I asked. "Don't you feel it sapping at your energy, having to maintain it?"

Freyja shrugged. "It is only another expenditure of energy. You get used to it after a while."

How many fae felt the same about their glamouring ability? How many other glamours did this city hold that most human never even learned about? The enormity of the power that sat beside me sipping his latte, hit me again. There was no way, I was letting Samuel work for anyone else, I thought.

"So, you glamoured Peter Grassi and his cabin near Manchac," I said.

Freyja looked startled that I knew about the cabin, but she nodded.

"What else?" I asked.

"Nothing else," Freyja said. "Mr. Bettencourt never asked for another thing from my fae abilities. He left me alone. I thought it was over, I thought I had just been fulfilling a favor of his for his friend. But then Lucy was taken."

Freyja rubbed at her face. "I didn't think it had anything to do with what I'd done, but then I heard you asking Mrs. Bettencourt about Peter Grassi and I knew Mr. Bettencourt had lied to his wife about seeing him recently, and I just—knew."

I nodded.

"Will you testify to this story under oath?" Samuel asked.

I opened my mouth to assure Freyja that he didn't mean it, that we would never ask her to, but Freyja spoke first.

"Yes," she said, quickly. "I owe it to Lucy. I owe it to Mrs. Bettencourt to tell the truth."

I didn't tell her that it probably wouldn't matter. The word of a fae, a lesser fae at that, against the word of a human who had donated faithfully to NOPD for years... I knew how that would turn out.

"Earlier today," I said. "Mr. Bettencourt had Mrs. Bettencourt committed. What happened?"

Freyja met my eyes. "I poisoned her."

Oh, it was as simple as that, huh? I heard Samuel shift in the seat beside me, leaning closer to the fae.

"You poisoned her?" he asked.

"Mr. Bettencourt had gotten a prescription of some kind from their doctor. He asked me to give it to Mrs. Bettencourt and that it would be better if 'she didn't know' she was receiving it." Freyja shook her head ruefully. "He didn't know that any fae worth her salt can recognize belladonna from a mile away. I couldn't give her something that could ruin her for life, make her more susceptible for whatever lies he put in her head, so I switched it out. I gave her a more mild sedative that caused the same effects, but short term. She'll recover and hopefully sue his ass into oblivion."

"You already intended to testify to this," I said. "You already planned to tell Mrs. Bettencourt everything."

Freyja nodded. "I am a good housekeeper. I am a hard worker. What Mr. Bettencourt did was wrong. Even I knew that."

It was a good story. It made sense, but I knew without evidence that NOPD couldn't ignore, that would be all it was. A story. We still needed to talk to Lucy.

"Tell me one last thing," I said. "Is Lucy Richard Bettencourt's daughter?"

Freyja gave a long-suffering sigh as though she had wrestled with the question herself. "I don't know."

I sipped from my coffee, the ice cubes clinking against one another at the movement.

"But I don't think Mr. Bettencourt thought she was."

And the motive just keeps piling on.

"Thank you, Freyja," I said. "I'm working on pulling a few more things together that might back up your story. Could you do me a favor and not tell Mrs. Bettencourt the truth just yet?"

Freyja gave me a long look. I could see the calculations she was making. "Okay, but I will not let her rot in some behavioral health facility. You have two days, and then I get her out of there and tell her everything." She stood to leave.

"Fair," I said. "One last request, though."

She paused.

"Drop the glamours," I said. "Both of them."

Freyja blinked once. "Done."

"Thank you."

Samuel watched the fae leave with eyes that missed nothing. "Do you think she was telling the truth?"

"Enough of it was," I said.

"No court will believe her," Samuel said.

"I know. Let's hope we can find some hard evidence to back her up."

"You mean?"

"Finish your latte. We're going to Manchac."

Freyja had been true to her word. The cabin on the shores of the Manchac appeared to me as it always had to Samuel. Slightly disheveled, but by no means uninhabitable. The sun was setting as we made the drive west. Samuel squinted into it and fiddled with the shades on the car until I told him to stop. I was the one driving, after all, and driver's in charge. Always.

Now, with the moon on the rise, we could see that there were no cars in front of the structure. Darryl must have somehow managed to tow his mangled silver beast away. I didn't imagine it would start up very nicely with the number of bullet holes that had covered its left side and hood, last I'd seen.

We parked a few houses away and approached on foot again, no cars in sight didn't necessarily mean that there was no one inside. We hadn't seen cars the last time we were here either.

The cabin was quiet as we approached. Whatever awaited us inside hadn't been alerted to our presence yet, or

I'm sure we would have been greeted with more lead than we wanted. The porch creaked under even my light weight, and we paused, listening for any movement inside. There was none, the absolute stillness of the air was almost eerie in the pale light of the rising moon.

It was the moment in every horror movie when the audience is screaming at the main character to not open that door, and the main character is a dumbass who opens the door anyway and then gets murdered in some gore-rific fashion. I turned the knob. It was me. I was the dumbass.

The door swung inward to absolute darkness. I had come prepared, packing supplies into my pockets from the dufflebag in the trunk. A knife in my right hand and a flashlight in my left. I was sure Samuel had his pistol in hand beside me, but I didn't waste a glance in his direction. When this was all over, I was going to make him teach me how to use one of those. The knife in my hand felt entirely inadequate for the situation.

The worn, wooden door let out an ungodly squeal on its hinges as it opened fully. I passed through the threshold and pressed myself against the wall beside the door before my silhouette in the doorway looked too inviting a target to whoever may lurk unseen in the dark.

Well, I had to shine a light on the room some time. Couldn't wait forever, no matter how inviting the splinters on the wall pressing into my back were. I clicked on the flashlight, bracing myself for the worst. The room was empty. A threadbare couch sat in the middle of the room facing a television that had a large splintering crack across the screen. A rug that looked as though it had never seen soap or water occupied the center of the floor, its original color completely indiscernible. Near the back wall was a stained wooden table that held a camping stove

Samuel bumped my shoulder, his gaze directing me toward the back of the one room shack. There, in the corner of the room, near the back door, sat a dog kennel. It was the only thing in this entire place that looked less than a decade old. The metal shone, reflecting the flashlight's beam. A threadbare red blanket lay inside. It was open now, the door swung against the wall, but I could see on the front of that door was a padlock that could only be opened with a key. You wouldn't need such measures if you were holding a dog. The whole no opposable thumbs thing was detriment enough to sliding the bars open, but a teenage girl? A scared teenage girl who had been kidnapped in the middle of the night? That you'd use a padlock for. I swallowed back the bile that rose in my throat.

The cage was only four feet long and maybe three feet tall, hardly enough for even a small sixteen-year-old to lie down comfortably. I crossed to the bars and lifted the lock with the edge of my blade. I wanted to smash the thing, to tear it off and throw it into the swamp outside, but I couldn't. There may be fingerprints on it. Hell, there may be evidence of Lucy having been here throughout this entire cabin.

"Don't touch anything," I said to Samuel, reasonably sure that there was no one nearby to hear us.

Samuel gave me a look as though I had offended his very nature. Right. He'd been a cop. He knew not to touch. I peeked my head out the back door, pushing the handle down with my elbow so as not to obstruct any prints there. The back porch held some fishing tackle, a few gasoline cans I assumed were empty. Whatever boat Peter Grassi had, it must have an engine on it. Good, if they came from the swamp, we would hear them approach just as surely as if they used a car.

I walked back into the main room. I didn't see Lucy's spirit anywhere, but I could sense *something*. Like hearing someone yell from far away, far enough that you couldn't pinpoint what direction the call came from. I closed my eyes and focused on the feeling, drawing her toward me. I reached down into the core of myself, the spark I felt behind my heart. The spark I'd neglected for nearly a decade.

"Lucy," I whispered into the room.

I opened my eyes as I felt Samuel shift beside me. No Lucy appeared.

I closed my eyes again and took a deep breath, filling my lungs, fanning the spark into a flame within me.

"*Lucy Bettencourt,*" the voice that came out of me was no longer my own. It was the voice of power. The voice of a Potesta. I felt her presence then, a prickle on the back of my neck, and snapped my eyes open. Lucy Bettencourt shrank into the corner of the room, as though she wanted to float through the wall and leave this place. I held her corporeal enough that she couldn't leave, but she still huddled against the wall, her eyes widened with fear as she peered around the room.

Samuel drew in a harsh breath beside me, and I knew I had brought her far enough into this physical plane that he could see her too. At the sound, Lucy looked at him and shrank back farther, seeming to fold in on herself as she cowered in the corner.

"Sammy," I whispered. "You've got to go."

"What?" He sounded dazed. I realized my hands were glowing from the summoning, a gold light that blazed through the room like a tiny sun. Shit, I had to figure out how to turn that off, anyone could probably see this cabin for miles.

"She's terrified of you," I said. "Go check outside. See if you can find anything Grassi left behind out there."

To his credit, Samuel didn't argue. He backed slowly out of the room, keeping his hands visible to the frightened spirit to show her he wasn't a threat. The instant the front door closed again Lucy relaxed.

"Wh-where am I," Lucy Bettencourt asked, her voice was hoarse. "Who are you?"

Florentina had told me that being pulled onto this plane would be disorienting for any ghost. Most spirits only saw shapes and shadows of the real world, from what I'd learned. She may not even remember what had happened, who had taken her, how she'd died. This may take some time.

Time for the hard part. "Lucy Bettencourt," I said. "I'm sorry to be the one to tell you this, but you're dead."

"I know that," the ghost snapped, her edges becoming even more solidified in her anger. Well, there's that teenage sass. Excuse me for trying the gentle approach. "What I mean is, what am I doing back here? In this place? Near that thing." She waved a hand toward the kennel.

"I brought you back here," I said.

She looked from my glowing arms to my face, studying me. Her eyes narrowed. "How?"

"It is what I do," I said. "I want to help you; I want to give you peace."

"There is no peace," Lucy's ghost whispered. "There is only pain and horror and nothingness."

Angsty. Hardcore. She could have played lead in any punk band in the city.

"You can have peace," I said. "There is more beyond this life. You can have rest. If you don't believe me, at least believe this, knowing what happened to you could give your mother peace." I took a chance. "Could give your father peace."

"He's not my father," Lucy snapped.

Ah, there it is. The final piece falling into place.

"Did your father do this to you?" I asked.

"I don't know."

Shit.

"Did Peter Grassi take you?"

Lucy flinched at the name. The edges of her face losing their hardened lines.

I softened my tone. "Who helped him? He couldn't have worked alone."

Lucy shook her head. "I don't know. I didn't recognize him."

"Can you tell me anything that will help us find him?" I asked. "Anything at all."

Lucy reached a hand to her throat; I could see the bruises there. Her hoarse voice made sense then. Broken blood vessels stood out red in her eyes as she remembered her death.

"I had a locket," she said. "The man I didn't know. He stole it from me."

"Would your mom recognize the locket if we found it?"

"She gave it to me," Lucy whispered.

The light from the summoning was slowly starting to fade, I noted. At least it wasn't permanent. That would be hard to explain. I could feel my abilities to hold Lucy on this plane fading with it. A bone deep exhaustion was settling in from the effort.

"Can you describe the other man?" I asked. "Hair, build, height, anything?"

Lucy was beginning to flicker in and out of physicality. Her face twisted in horror. I didn't want to let her go back to that place of nothingness she'd talked about. I wanted to keep her here, to keep her safe, not frightened while we worked to bring her peace.

She flickered back once, twice. Her spirit raised a finger, pointing over my shoulder.

"Him."

She disappeared.

I turned, raising my hands, raising my knife, but a fist across the jaw knocked me to the ground and the blade spun out of my hands and off into the darkness.

"Sammy!" I yelled. Fighting in the dark was real far down my list of desired scenarios. If I survived this, I would certainly be getting an earful from Master Harnock about it.

Two massive hands clasped around my throat, and I beat at them with both fists trying to break his hold.

"Sammy can't hear you," the voice hissed, right in my face a noseful of foul breath making me gag.

The edges of my sight were growing fuzzy, even in the dark room, like television static encroaching on my vision. Shit, I was going to die here.

My lips were turning numb, my hands scrabbling uselessly against the man's hold. What had happened to Sammy? Where the hell was he?

One last thought occurred to me: he better be dead, or I was certainly going to haunt his ass.

Then, my brain gave itself over to the darkness and I was pulled under.

# Chapter Fourteen

It was dark. Completely dark. Something lay over my face, almost smothering me, but not quite. I twisted my head trying to dislodge whatever was impeding my vision. I was able to catch sight of a flash of gray somewhere below my chin. A hood, or a bag of some kind. Not a blindfold, then. I focused on my breathing. In. Out. Listen. Feel.

The sound of waves no larger than ripples lapping against a shore, met my ears. A hard wood dug into my back. My hands were bound behind me using something. I felt around the binding. Rope. A strong rope. Shit. They'd tied my wrists to one of the bollards of the dock, leading out to the bayou.

Two different voices, getting nearer. They were pissed.

"What do you mean she's still alive?" Peter Grassi's voice.

"She was unconscious, what did you want me to do, kill her?" The man who had attacked me in the cabin.

"Yes, Bud," Grassi said. "I was assured that wouldn't be

a problem when I hired you. You seemed more than capable of taking care of the girl."

Ah, a confession. Too bad you're going to die here and can't tell anyone, a voice in my mind whispered. Not if I could help it. Not a chance in hell was I letting some asshole named Bud get the better of me.

I shifted my weight as evenly as I could, praying the dock wouldn't creak under me. Hoping they weren't looking my direction. The handle of the knife in my boot dug into the side of my calf. He hadn't even searched me? Bud was just as dumb as he sounded. Now if I could only draw my leg up, maybe I could get ahold of the blade.

"We could dump her in the bayou," Bud's voice said. "Let the rusalki take care of her."

Oh, would you? I wanted to beg, yes please. I could feel the water calling to me as he spoke.

"No guarantee the rusalki would come," Grassi said. *Dammit.*

"They like blood."

A thoughtful noise. "That they do."

I could hear their footsteps on the dock, getting closer. I counted the paces until they were beside where I sat on the hard damp wood. I had to be near the end of the dock, I surmised. The water right below me. So close.

"Is she awake?" Bud asked.

A sharp toe of a boot dug into my thigh. "Wake up," Grassi said.

I moaned as though I was just coming to. They didn't need to know how much of their conversation I had heard. "Wh-what happened?" I asked. I added a note of panic to my voice. "Where am I?"

"Shut up," Grassi said. I felt him reaching around me to my arms. A sharp sting as he drew a blade across my forearm. Hot blood dripped down my hands, wetting the knots that bound me. I heard it falling to the water below.

"There," Grassi said. "That should do the trick?"

"She's pretty," Bud said. "Shame we can't keep her."

"There's a bag over her head." Grassi snapped.

"Yeah," Bud said. His voice was much closer to my face as he clarified. "But the rest of her is pretty."

I tried not to gag as a meaty hand dropped onto my shoulder. Its heavy dampness drew down across my chest. I could feel the heat radiating off his body as he loomed over me. I sent a wild kick his direction, hoping to connect with something.

My efforts were rewarded with a swear of pain. A hand slapped across my face, stinging my cheek through the thin fabric that covered my head. I drew in a hiss.

"You bitch," Bud snarled. "I oughta—"

I drew back against the post as his body heat left my side and I had no way of knowing where he stood. Or where Peter Grassi stood for that matter. They could be anywhere, preparing to strike or kick or slit my throat. I swallowed.

Then I heard it.

A faint splashing behind me, drawing closer. I could *feel* them behind me. Their predatory presence in the water. Even the insects ceased buzzing at their advance. All of the bayou seemed to be holding its breath to see what happened next. I held my breath right along with it.

I jumped as a high-pitched shriek sounded. Even *I* wanted to cover my ears. They were so close to the dock, the waves their movements created lapped up the sides, spraying me with water. I heard the two pairs of feet pounding up the dock. Away from me. Away from the rusalki they had teased with my blood.

Idiots. The rusalki couldn't leave the water. They

weren't like the melusines they had been exiled from. They had forgotten how to change back to their human form, how to breathe the air of this world. Their bloodlust filled them with rage for what they couldn't reach, and more water sprayed my back at their splashing fury. They wanted me. Badly. At least, they thought they did. I clenched my teeth; they didn't know what they were asking for.

With the two men giving me space, I drew my right leg up toward me again, reaching my fingers down toward my boot. The bindings on my wrists dug into my skin as I strained against them. I could barely feel the tip of the knife handle. Contorting my body sideways, gave me an extra inch or so and I had it! I whipped the blade around and started sawing through the rope.

Then the footsteps returned, accompanied by hurried voices as though they had just realized that the rusalki couldn't advance on me. They stopped at the edge of the dock, too afraid to come closer to the water and the beasts that thrashed under its surface. Ha, stay there, I thought. I just needed a few more seconds and—

A splash covered my body. Not from the water this time, from the direction of the shoreline. A harsh chemical smell filled my nostrils and I gasped for air. My hood was soaked, my clothes were soaked. My brain seemed to short-circuit trying to place the scent overwhelming my senses. Then, I heard the distinctive sound of a match catching and my brain helpfully supplied the word it had been looking for. Gasoline. Shit, shit, shit.

I sawed through the last of the bindings just as my hood caught aflame. I ripped the fabric from my head and threw it away into the water, my hands stinging. The gas had soaked through to my face and my skin was on fire, the smell of burning hair filling my nostrils. I twisted my body like an acrobat in one last effort to get away from the flames that were crawling up my clothes. I curved through the air and off the dock to the relief of the water.

And to the monsters who waited below.

August nights never really cooled off this far south. We were lucky if we could sport a light jacket in the evening this time of year. The waters feeding into the bayous and swamps had a tendency to hold onto their heat, a cloying warmth that was the perfect breeding ground for all the strange animals that called it home. The Manchac would never be described as cold, but compared to the inferno I left on the dock, it was positively refreshing.

I transformed the second I hit the water. My legs kicking off the pants that would have kept them apart, an itching sensation spreading down them as the surrounding water called the iridescent blue and green scales forth. I drew a rush of water into my lungs, cooling the burns that trailed through my respiratory system. The gills on my ribcage easily blew the water out and away once it had done its work.

I could sense the rusalki from the dock enough that I knew they were there, but I couldn't have pinpointed their exact locations. Now that I was in the water with them, I could sense them entirely. I knew that there were four of them, a larger number than were often seen together. I knew that two of them were injured, desperate for food and healing. And I knew how far away each one was from where I landed in the water.

I had nearly landed on one of them as I crashed through the surface and it raked its clawed fingers down my chest, shredding what was left of my burnt t-shirt, as I descended before it. The face before me was twisted in hunger and madness. The pale skin looking sickly as nearly non-existent lips pulled back from a mouthful of sharpened fangs.

I bared my own teeth in response and saw a flicker of recognition in the rusalka's face before it decided to take a chance and moved toward me in the water. I kicked it back once before it could sink its teeth into me and drew in a breath of water. I poured every ounce of power, every ounce of my birthright through my voice.

*"Get the fuck back."*

The rusalki gave a collective shriek as the sound and power of my siren-call commanded them away. I was sure their screams could be heard on the shore, and I hoped the two men who had tried to kill me assumed that it was the sound of my burnt body being eaten. I sent a burst of power toward the gathered rusalki with a whip of my tail. The fin cut through the muddy bayou water with nothing short of a thunderclap.

The lot of them quickly decided that I was not the food they were looking for, and they wheeled away from me. I wished a could have helped them. That I could have healed them and given them food. It was the bleeding heart of my heritage, that urge to protect what had once been my own. But I couldn't now. I had to send them away. *I* had to get away.

I dropped as close to the floor of the bayou as my tail would allow and turned away from the dock. I shook off the remnants of my shirt and stretched my body as far as I could in the water, relishing the feeling of freedom. Here, I didn't have to pretend to be human. I didn't have to be something I wasn't. Here I could be what I was born to be. Melusine. Free.

I'd put nearly a mile between myself and the dock before I chanced a surfacing. My head poked out into the night air, the warm humidity feeling almost the same against the skin of my face and breasts as the water had. My eyesight was heightened in my true form. The dark was no challenge for me now and I could see up the shore toward the cabin where the dock still smoldered. Two figures stood near its smoking frame, peering into the water. The houses lining the shore may as well have been abandoned for the lack of movement I saw inside them. I could see our abandoned car between two of the shacks, a dented pickup truck parked behind it. Where was Samuel? Had they really killed him before attacking me?

I could have made a break for the car while Grassi and his henchman were distracted, but the water and my melusine form served to speed up the healing process and I wasn't quite ready to give that up. A flick of my tail sent me farther up the shore, and I let the water rushing past me cool the burns on my chest and face, bringing healing and refreshment. For a while I let the current carry me along. The spirit of the water directing my path.

I surfaced again a few moments later. I was closer to our car now. The truck was still parked behind it. I was sure that meant the two men were still occupied. Were they still looking out into the bayou, or had they returned to the inside of the shack? Were they destroying evidence as I sat in the water, enjoying myself? That thought spurred me forward, and I pulled myself from the water. I shook the dripping bayou from my arms, my tail transforming back into two distinct legs, the scales disappearing from their surface. I stood in the warm night air, wringing my hair between my hands.

"You're—you're—"

My head snapped around at the sound of the voice and I brought my hands up, ready to fight. Samuel stood a few paces away, his jaw slack as he stared at me.

I looked down at my naked torso, the water dripping from my hair down my arms and legs.

"Can I borrow your shirt?"

Samuel swallowed once, his eyes large in the moonlight. He slipped his shirt off without a word and I pulled it over my own head. I was suddenly grateful that my shorter frame meant that the shirt that stopped at his waist, covered me to mid-thigh.

"Peter Grassi and one other man are at the cabin," I said, quickly. "I'm afraid by the time we get back with anyone who can help, they'll have destroyed whatever evidence of Lucy might have been there."

Samuel still didn't speak, but he nodded once. I could see his eyes constantly drifting to my legs and then away. How much did he see, I wondered. Had he caught a glimpse of scales and gills and fin?

"I'm going to go make sure they're too well occupied to even consider cleaning up after their crime," I said. "Any chance you could disable the truck? Make it undriveable? Shoot it maybe?"

I saw Samuel's Adam's apple bob in a swallow. "You're one of them," he whispered. "The beings this city fears the most and you're one of them."

I wound my hair up into a knot behind my head.

"If you tell anyone about this," I said. "I'll sic your grandmother on you. Understand?"

Samuel's eyes widened even larger than I thought possible, but he nodded again.

"Good," I said. "Let's go."

I left Samuel at the car. I couldn't waste time waiting for him to figure out how to disable the pickup truck and I didn't really need him seeing what I'd do to keep the two men who'd killed Lucy occupied.

I'd gone through a list of possibilities in my mind. It would be too difficult to keep them out of the cabin while we were gone. I didn't see us being able to subdue the two of them and throw them in the trunk of my car. Not when only Samuel knew how to shoot, and both the men were certainly armed to the teeth. There was only one method I could use to guarantee they wouldn't be able to mar the crime scene and I hated to use it.

Talking to Lucy had set off the beacon to every ghost in the area that a Potesta was nearby. My transformation in the water seemed to have held them back, confused them maybe. Now that I was jogging along the shoreline completely human and cursing my lost boots as my feet sank into bayou muck, they gathered.

Five had met me here the last time. Now, rows upon rows of them hovered over the water, watching my movements. Control my fear, control the spirits, I told myself. I took deep breaths to slow the pounding of my heart. Watching those spirits, staring at me, hungering after me, I was sixteen again. I blinked back memories of horror and pain.

I wasn't a little kid anymore, I told myself. I could do this. What was it Samuel had said? Fake it 'til you make it? Here goes nothing.

I steeled myself, clenching my fists, calling on the power that sat behind my breastbone. My arms began to glow as I called to the spirits who had gathered.

*"Come."*

The ghosts fell into line behind me, a trail of spirits of all shapes and sizes. Elderly, youths, middle aged. Those who had been killed in hurricanes. Those who had been eaten by the creatures that called the bayou home. It was a veritable army of souls descending on two unsuspecting assholes.

The two men had been crouched on the edge of the water, searching its surface for movement, for a body, for anything that would indicate that I was well and truly dead.

"Hey asshat," I called.

Peter Grassi stood at my voice and turned to face me. "Damn it, Bud. I knew the rusalki weren't a guarantee of anything."

The other man rose beside Grassi. His face and arms were lined with scars and tattoos. His head was shaved clean, but a graying goatee held onto his chin. A belly hung over his stained jeans, barely held in by a white tank top.

"That's okay," he said. The menace in his voice was palpable. "If she's dumb enough to come back here, she's dumb enough that people will believe she stumbled into the bayou and drowned."

Bud took a step around Peter Grassi and advanced toward me, his boots sucking against the mud with each step.

"Ah, ah, ah," I said. "I wouldn't do that if I were you. My friends might be pissed."

Bud looked around with exaggeration. "I don't see no friends."

I clenched my fists, my arms springing into a glow of gold that nearly turned the shoreline to daylight as I pulled the army behind me onto this physical plane.

"How about now?" I asked sweetly.

Peter Grassi was already backing onto the dock, his eyes wide and wild at the sight. Bud took an involuntary step back before changing his mind and drawing a blade from behind his back. It was a wicked, curving thing, a hunting knife.

I shook my head. "Oh, you don't want to do that," I said.

"Come on," Bud said, his face turning near purple in his rage. "You want a fight, let's fight."

He brandished the blade my direction. I smiled. A direct threat meant he was fair game. The death of a man who murdered little girls wouldn't weigh on my conscience too heavily.

I looked to the two spirits that flanked me, a young man who was probably in his early twenties when he'd passed and a woman who could have been his mother.

"*Kill*," I ordered.

Bud's eyes widened as the two descended on him. He lashed out with his knife, but the blade passed right through the spirit of the woman. The young man surged forward. I tried to hide my unease as the ghost disappeared *into* the man before me.

The bald man froze. The blade fell from his hand. Frost crawled across his skin. His eyes, wide with shock and fear, clouded over as ice crossed their surface. One puff of frosty air left his lungs and he toppled to the ground, his body shattering against the wood of the dock.

Well, that was horrifying. Didn't know they could do that.

Peter Grassi huddled at the end of the dock. The wood had stopped smoldering, but a slight smoke still lingered in the air from where they had tried to burn me. His hands shook as he held them out before him. "Stay back," he said. "I don't know what you want but stay back."

I gestured with my glowing arms and the ghosts surrounded the dock. They stood along the shore and hovered over the water creating a wall around the wooden structure. There was nowhere for Peter Grassi to go.

"They won't touch you if you stay on the dock," I called. I demonstrated by allowing the ghosts to blink out of sight and then pulling them back to physicality in the same location they'd left.

"What do you want?" Peter asked.

"Justice for the girl you murdered."

"I didn't touch her," Grassi said. "My hands are clean."

"We'll let the courts determine that," I said. "Stay on the dock and you'll be safe. The authorities will be by soon to collect you."

Peter Grassi looked uneasily around the dock. "That's it? You're not going to kill me?"

"Not my job," I said. "Like I said, we'll let the lawyers sort it out. Although I'm sure they'll give you a nice plea deal if you tell them just how involved Richard Bettencourt was in his daughter's kidnapping and murder."

Peter Grassi's eyebrows rose. He hadn't thought I knew about that.

I let the spirits blink out of sight again. "They're still there," I warned him. "Stay on the dock and they won't touch you."

Peter nodded. He lowered himself to the dock, sitting cross legged on the hard wood. He was settling in for the wait, I realized. A good sign. I couldn't hold the spirits here while Samuel and I drove back to the city, but Peter Grassi didn't need to know that.

Satisfied that he wouldn't move, I turned back to the road. Samuel stood near the porch of the cabin, watching me warily. I shook the glow off my arms and walked past him toward the car.

As I passed the windows of the cabin, I saw a small face appear. Something tugged in my heart as I watched Lucy Bettencourt's spirit mouth 'thank you' and disappear again.

I blinked at the stinging in my eyes and got into the passenger side of the car. Samuel didn't speak, didn't question. He took his seat behind the wheel and turned the car around on the narrow dirt road.

As we passed the pickup truck that Samuel had disabled, I saw a glow in the cab. There hanging from the rearview mirror, reflecting the moonlight as though it produced a glow of its own, was a locket on a gold chain.

# Chapter Fifteen

"In a surprising turn of events, Louisa Bettencourt has been released from the Crescent City Mental Health Institute the same day her *husband* was arrested as a person of interest in their daughter's kidnapping and murder." The anchor woman's voice was a pleasant change to the mother henning I'd been receiving from Florentina and Brigitte. I lay on my back on Brigitte's cold examination table, my head turned toward the small television as the image shifted to shaky camera footage and uniformed officers approaching Peter Grassi's cabin. "We now have a view from our cameras on the ground of New Orleans Police Department officers cordoning off a cabin near Manchac where they believe Lucy Bettencourt was held for days before she was murdered. The student from Crescent City Academy was just three weeks from her seventeenth birthday when her body was found strangled and left on her parent's lawn."

I turned my face away from the screen as school photos of Lucy flashed across it. I looked up into the bright lights of Brigitte's workroom and blinked.

"Stay on this channel for all the updates for this absolute tragedy."

Florentina clicked the TV off as the newscaster began straightening her papers and an incoming commercial break threatened.

"You should be using Renauld's method," my aunt said. She was at my side again, peering down at the work Brigitte was performing with a hawkish gaze.

"Renauld's would be faster, but it would lead to more scarring," Brigitte said softly. "I'm relatively certain that since Meranda's life is not currently in danger from the burns, she would like me to take my time and give her the best chance of breathing without the difficulty of scar tissue impeding rib expansion."

My aunt gave a huff and sounded as though she was about to reply, but Brigitte cut her off.

"With all due respect Madame LaMontagne, you are a guest in my house, in my workroom. Please step back."

I gave Florentina an apologetic look but was secretly relieved that I hadn't had to be the one to kick her out. My aunt to her credit drew herself up with supreme dignity and stalked from the room.

"Thank you," I whispered.

"Hold still," Brigitte said.

I placed a hand on her arm closest to me. She stilled the moves she was making over my face and neck where the burns had turned the olive skin an abhorrent shade of maroon.

"I mean it, Brigitte," I said. "Thank you. For everything."

"Don't think I'm not pissed at you for getting yourself into this state," my best friend said. For an instant her calm demeanor cracked, and her fear leaked through. "But I will fix you. Every time."

"I know," I said. "I'm sorry."

Brigitte shook my hand off and returned to her work, hovering her hands over the surface of my chest. Their soft glow bathed my chest in a cool sensation that made me want to shiver. "It won't happen again," Brigitte said. "Once you sell the Agency, you won't be out there killing yourself on a case and then beating my door down in the middle of the night for healing."

I craned my neck to look at the work she was performing. "You're so good at this," I said. It was an old habit of ours. She'd ask questions I knew she wouldn't like the answer to, and I'd distract her with compliments. "It would hardly be fair to hold work back from an artist."

Brigitte placed a hand on my forehead and pushed my head back down to the thin pillow it had been resting on.

"You *are* still selling the Agency, aren't you?"

"You're very pretty."

"Dang it, Mer!"

"It's true!" I insisted. "The way the light catches your hazel eyes in this room, the glow from your hands. You're like an angel. A perfect, beautiful, healing angel."

"You're the worst," Brigitte said, smacking my shoulder lightly.

"Ow, I'm injured." I said jutting out my lower lip in what I was sure was an offensively comical pout.

She worked in silence for a while. I didn't know the name of the method she was using, but it certainly took a long while. She'd been up most of the night with me and only half the burns on my chest had been changed to the soft pink of new skin. I was sure I was exhausting her, but she didn't complain. She never complained about her work.

"I can't sell it," I said softly. "Dad gave me the Agency for a reason, and I think I'm starting to understand a little better."

"You were always good at it," Brigitte said. Her words an agreement, a peace treaty. "Even when you were younger and didn't know anything. You were good with the people."

"Now I'm older and I still don't know anything," I said.

"Yes, but you *know* that about yourself," she said. "Much different from when we were teenagers."

I laughed. She was right. Funny that you could know absolutely everything with such intense certainty as a youth and then a few years later, be an intellectual invalid.

The door opened and Samuel walked into the room. He made an awful squawking sound and slapped a hand over his eyes. "Boobs," he said.

"It's not like you haven't seen them before," I said.

Brigitte gave me a look and I shook my head at her. She narrowed her eyes at me, all suspicion and protectiveness. I gave her a grin.

"What's up, Sammy?" I asked.

He kept his hand firmly placed over his eyes as he spoke. "Phone call came for you," he held my cell phone out and I strained to take it from his hand. "A Jill Logan."

I snatched the phone, nearly falling off the examination table to the sound of Brigitte's hiss of displeasure.

I gave her an apologetic look as I pressed the phone to my ear. "Meranda Haley."

"Ms. Haley," Secretary Logan's voice was awfully chipper for a Tuesday morning. "Ms. Holden will be out for the next few days, any chance you're looking for some substituting time?"

I couldn't hold back the grin that spread across my face. "I think I could fill in. See you tomorrow morning?"

"Tomorrow morning, Ms. Haley," Jill said. I could hear the smile in her voice before she hung up the phone.

I tossed the phone back across the room toward Samuel. It hit him in the chest and ricocheted to the floor. Huh, guess he hadn't been peeking. That or he was a suspiciously committed liar. Samuel stooped to grab the phone and left the room so fast I was almost sure he closed the door on himself.

"You're back?" Brigitte asked.

"I'm back."

"Agency too?"

I blew out a breath of air at the enormity of what I was committing to but nodded. "Agency too."

"Great, I'm happy for you. Now hold still."

"Yes, ma'am."

# Epilogue

My favorite place at the bar was empty when I walked into Baxter's that evening. I slid onto the barstool beside the sleeping pup and scratched behind his ears. A contented rumble sounded in the bulldog's chest at my ministrations, interrupting his snore.

I'd tied my brown hair back off my neck, giving the new skin a chance to breathe in the open air. From below my chin, almost to the bottom of my sternum, my skin was pink and soft. Baby's skin Brigitte had called it. It was sensitive and the thought of covering it up with clothing that could scratch against the new flesh had made me want to dive back into a swamp, so I opted for a blouse whose neckline plunged low between my breasts.

It wasn't something I would wear on the town every night, but it served its purpose tonight. Here in the back corner of Baxter's, no one would be bold enough to approach me. I'd had to come here tonight. I had something to prove to myself.

The drive back from Manchac, my arms had shaken. It

wasn't just the burns; it was the adrenaline. It was the real-ization of the power I had just wielded and the absolute exhaustion it had left in its wake. I needed more practice if I planned on making a living with Dad's Agency. My Agency.

Charlie appeared before me, startling me from my thoughts.

"You look nice," he said.

"Thanks," I said. "I try to dress up for Baxter."

The bulldog in question rolled over and let out a huff of repulsively scented air.

Charlie chuckled. "Your usual?"

"Not today, Charlie," I said. "I think I'm in the mood for a rum."

Charlie's eyebrows rose and he placed a hand on his chest. "I never thought I'd see the day,"

"Keep it up and I'll change my mind," I said.

"Coming right up," Charlie said quickly, spinning on his heel and walking to the middle of the bar where the expensive bottles stood behind the counter on a raised plat-form in all their glory. It looked like a tiny mountain of booze and regret. I'd never once dared to climb it in this place. But the spirits of the city remained outside the bar doors. Florentina had cleansed me of my draw for them with a threat that she wouldn't help again. I'd have to figure it out for myself next time. I think she was a little upset that she'd been kicked out of the healing room.

I wasn't scared. I'd taken a degree of power I hadn't known I'd possessed and used it without hurting anyone I hadn't intended to. It was time to take the next step. I would learn everything Tante Flora could teach me. I'd let Samuel take me to a firearms range. I'd even have Master Harnock show me how to not get knocked off my feet in a fight. But not tonight. Tonight, I would drink. For the first time in years.

Charlie came back with a tumbler of amber liquid. He watched as I held the concoction to my nose and gave it a swirl, breathing in the dark spicy scent.

"It's not a wine," the bartender grunted. "You don't need to woo it."

I laughed and waved him away. "Let me enjoy myself in peace."

Baxter gave a loud snore beside me, shattering whatever illusion I had that peace would reign once Charlie left, but the bartender obediently wandered off to check on other customers.

I took a sip of my drink and closed my eyes as the liquid burned pleasantly down my throat. It felt like a fire had lit somewhere in my abdomen, not an entirely unpleasant sensation. The new skin on my chest and neck left me almost cold despite the August evening air, and the rum served to warm me from the inside.

I felt a presence beside me and snapped my eyes open. A man sat on the barstool beside me. It wasn't a spirit. I could feel them wandering the streets outside the bar, but none had chanced a venture into the barroom tonight.

He looked to be about my age, maybe a few years older. A few days unshaven. I wouldn't call his facial hair a beard yet, but it was leaning that direction. His blond hair was long enough to show light waves, but not so long as to be shaggy. His blue eyes were fixed on the mirror above the bar, watching something outside.

I followed his gaze to see a new set of spirits gathered outside of the main doors of the bar. There was no one else there. But the ghosts couldn't be what he was staring at, could they?

I looked past him at the row of empty barstools he had bypassed to sit on the one beside me.

"Can I help you?" I asked.

He turned to face me, his eyes a piercing ice blue. He smelled of salt air, as though he had just come from the gulf. His cotton shirt was white and clean its neckline revealing well-tanned skin that matched his face and arms. I wondered absentmindedly how much time he spent in the sun without any kind of shirt. His dark pants looked almost leather in the dull light of the bar, but that didn't make any sense. No one wore leather pants unless they were a rebellious vampire youth or a rock star. The tan ruled out the vampire option and those scars and callouses on his hands did not come from guitar playing. They came from hard work, building or fighting maybe.

His blue eyes dropped down to the chasm of skin that ran almost to my belly button. I felt my heart quicken under his gaze.

"This is new," he murmured. Before I could stop him, he'd placed a warm finger in the center of my sternum. His touch was gentle, but my skin screamed, the nerve endings new and cranky. He must have seen something of what I felt in my face. He drew back as though I had burned him.

"Did you need something?" I asked. I prayed that my cheeks weren't as red as I felt they might be.

"Not yet," he said. Great, the guy's a cryptic. "I'll find you if I do."

That wasn't creepy at all. I drew my shoulders back, straightening my spine and granting myself a confidence I seemed to have lost when the newcomer sat down.

"There are plenty of other places you could be sitting," I pointed out. "I'd thank you to pick one of them."

A hint of a smile touched the man's face, setting off a

dimple that had been hidden beneath the day's old scruff. He rose from the stool beside me leaving behind the scent of the ocean, the Gulf I hadn't visited since I was sixteen. A memory that the melusine part of me longed for, where my kind had lived for years. I closed my eyes against the smell, breathing it in without apology.

"See you around, Meranda," he whispered. The harsh smell of cigar smoke on his breath pulled me from my reverie and I opened my eyes, but he was gone.

The door beside the bar was swinging closed. He'd opted not to leave through the front where the spirits had gathered. Interesting.

I took another sip of my rum and scratched Baxter's head. I had questions, too many questions. His last words had sounded like a promise.

But tonight, I didn't need answers. The questions would keep 'til morning.

Tonight, I had a drink to finish and an overweight bulldog to pet.

All else could wait.

# Acknowledgments

There are so many people I'd like to thank for helping to make this book all it could be.

Firstly, Eloise, my amazing critique partner, thank you for putting up with all of the rambling and the typos and the late night messages.

Selina, for being so willing to answer my nagging questions whatever they may be. You inspire me.

My editor, Katie, for taking a chance on me.

Kevin J. Anderson for convincing me to hit the publish button. You were right.

Mark Leslie Lefebvre for reminding me to never reject myself.

My family for putting up with everything.

My readers, it's all for you.

Love to you all.

*Soli Deo Gloria*

# About the Author

*jjlynndaniels.com*

Starting out as a voracious reader in a desert in Southern California, JJ Lynn Daniels escaped the heat to become a stay-at-home author living within view of the Rocky Mountains of the western United States.

When not writing books, raising her three daughters, teaching her German Shepherd mix new tricks, or working as a registered nurse, JJ likes to sit on the back porch with a hot cup of coffee and a good book.

JJ Lynn Daniels is the author of The Metal's Bane Series and The Meranda Haley Series.

# About the Publisher

B. Shepherd Publications LLC was formed in 2022 by founder JJ Lynn Daniels. The imprint specializes in stories that build resiliency and antifragility in their readers.

May resistance make you stronger.

B. Shepherd Publication's flagship author is JJ Lynn Daniels.

bshepherdpublications.com